I0553312

TEXAS COWBOY MARSHAL

BARB HAN

TorJake Publishing

Copyright © 2022 by Barb Han

All rights reserved.

No part of this book may be reproduced in any form or by any electronic or mechanical means, including information storage and retrieval systems, without written permission from the author, except for the use of brief quotations in a book review.

Editing: Ali Williams

Cover Design: Jacob's Cover Designs

To my family for unwavering love and support. I can't imagine doing life with anyone else.

CHAPTER ONE

The tiny hairs on the back of Naomi Martin's neck pricked as she prepared to exit the Ford Escape she'd parked in the hospital lot where she worked. She and several other nightshift nurses had already brought a complaint to management about the lack of lighting, so she didn't immediately switch her lights off. Clocking in at eleven at night meant it was dark outside when her shift started all year round, perfect cover for the secret admirer who'd been leaving 'gifts' on her car while she worked.

Naomi glanced around, looking for any sign of movement; when she saw none, she turned off her head-lights. Nothing ever prepared her for the moment she was plunged into the pitch-black darkness. She'd parked as close to the ER as humanly possible, and the parking lot was fairly full for a Tuesday night. At least the ER had the most activity going on. In the worst instance, there was a chance someone would hear her screams.

Tonight, everything was quiet save for the wind as she exited and locked her vehicle.

Crisp fall gusts whipped her hair around; the ends felt like needles against her skin. She tightened her grip on the top of her jacket. It hadn't been cold enough for a full-on coat yet but the chill in the air said that was about change.

Tucking her chin to her chest to stave off the chill, she marched toward the set of double glass doors in the distance, scanning the area while keen to pay attention to her peripheral vision. It would be so easy to surprise her from the side of one of the many vehicles. To give herself a chance at escape, she walked straight down the center line of the lane, so if someone jumped out at her, she would have a couple of seconds head start. Those few seconds might mean the difference between life and death. At least she was able to wear tennis shoes to work. She couldn't imagine making this trek in a pair of heels. Although, it occurred to her a spiked heel could be used as a weapon.

That feeling of eyes on her back stalked her all the way inside the building. She thought about the U.S. Marshal who'd been brought in last night. Maybe she could ask his opinion off the record? The man might be drop-dead gorgeous, but he was also a good resource. Once the glass doors swished closed, she exhaled. This was the second time this week she'd had that feeling. Campus security was stretched thin, or she would have at least considered calling for an escort. Then again Rod, the night guard, wasn't exactly her favorite person. The last time she'd asked him to arrange for more lighting, he'd asked her why she needed it when cars now had timers on their head-lights. She didn't bother to point out that not everyone could afford new car payments. Some people had to drive older vehicles.

Aggravation caused Naomi's shoulders to tense. She shook it off. She was about to start a long shift and work would consume her soon enough, forcing out all other thoughts. Her mind briefly shifted to the U.S. Marshal on her floor as she moved toward the elevator bank. She pushed the button to floor number seven and wondered if he might have some helpful advice for her. She was drawing a blank on how seriously she should take the gifts and how panicked she should be. The whole ordeal might be nothing to worry about, and she might be overreacting as Rod had indicated. Or, maybe she should get the law involved.

As the elevator doors closed, a male hand came out of seemingly nowhere, forcing them open again. She gasped, hating the fact that she'd been caught off guard by something that happened all the time.

The doors sprang open and Theo walked in.

"Hey, Theo," Naomi said, trying to shake off the bout of nerves.

The orderly from her floor was quiet as usual. He gave a slight nod while keeping his gaze locked onto the floor. Theo packed his lunch every day, although some guessed his mother or a caregiver did it for him, and it was presently attached to a crossbody strap. The rare times he'd actually spoken to Naomi, she realized he had a slight stutter and she thought he might be self-conscious about it. She always went out of her way to make him feel welcome on her floor.

"Seven?" she asked, knowing it was his usual first stop.

Theo gave another quick nod as he shoved his hands in his pockets. His toes were almost pointed toward each other as he stood there. But his small smile let her know he appreciated her kindness. The few times he'd spoken to her, she'd noticed a stutter and he seemed insecure about it.

The seventh floor couldn't get there fast enough for Naomi. She didn't mind Theo, but she was ready to dig into work and forget about the creepiness from the parking lot. Thankfully, the ride ended up a straight shot with no interruptions. Naomi could count on one hand the number of times that had happened this month. Maybe this shift would turn around after all.

The elevator's chime broke into the awkward silence. Theo immediately shuffled out the instant the doors opened. He threw back a hand in an attempt at a wave.

"Have a good shift," she said to him, following with enough distance to give him space before splitting off in the opposite direction.

The creepy eyes-on-her feeling still plagued her. It was the worst feeling and one she wished she could shed. Ever since a 'secret admirer' had left a dead rose on her windshield, she'd had that feeling. Not long after, a stuffed teddy bear holding a heart had shown up on her vehicle. Then, after another long night at work last week, a silk robe waited for her tucked underneath her windshield wiper. Her body involuntarily shivered at the memory.

Talking to Rod in security had been absolutely no

help. He'd laughed at her concerns before telling her the gestures were nothing more than a sign someone probably had a crush on her and she should stop being so uptight. That was the moment she realized hospital security was probably not going to be any help and there was no chance Rod was losing his keycard to the 'good ole boys' club anytime soon.

At the moment, Naomi wasn't seriously dating anyone and hadn't been on a promising date in longer than she cared to admit. She was even more embarrassed by the fact that she'd let Rita, her co-worker, talk her into signing up for one of those dating sites so Naomi could move on.

After a third—not just bad but horrific—date, Naomi had pulled her profile down and changed her status on social media to *in a relationship* to kill anyone's expectation they might get a follow-up date. The lie seemed harmless enough and she had no plans of dating for the foreseeable future.

Now that her thirtieth birthday had come and gone unceremoniously, she had no plans to date anyone. If dating in her twenties had been complicated, the next decade wasn't off to a real good start either.

The gifts on her vehicle probably shouldn't have freaked her out as much as they had, but it just didn't sit well with her. Was it the secrecy? Yes, of course, that was part of it. The dead rose was creepy. Rod had explained people used to iron them and keep them inside books. His aunt had shown him several that she used as bookmarks over the years. He'd rolled his eyes and issued a sharp sigh before picking up a file on his desk, essentially dismissing her. Again, she wondered if the Marshal would see the situation in the same light.

And yet, what purpose did the gifts serve if she had no idea who'd left them? A dead flower. A teddy bear. A silk robe. They followed a normal dating progression in a sense, becoming more intimate each time. But also creepy considering the secrecy. If someone was trying to impress her, wouldn't they leave a card with a name instead of slinking around in the dark? Especially since this location away from the hustle and bustle of Austin wasn't exactly easy to get to.

This hospital might be named Austin General but it was on the outskirts of town. She'd chosen this place to work so that she didn't have to wrestle with the city's traffic, which was a nightmare. There was no rush 'hour' in Austin; every hour was rush hour. Working and living in the outskirts had its pluses. However, there was still a good ole boy network that got by too easily, too unnoticed. No one called them out, including hospital administration. No one took it seriously, which was a problem. It was considered harmless, which was infuriating. Rod needed to take her concerns about the parking lot seriously before someone got hurt. Instead, he'd promised to figure out a way to get more lighting at the edges of the lot, giving a vague timeline.

Naomi logged in and located fellow nurse Rita, whose shift would end now that Naomi had arrived.

"How'd it go today?" Naomi asked, suppressing the urge to dive right in and ask about the Marshal who'd come in yesterday. He'd caused quite a stir on the floor when the famous Texas cattle ranching family had filed in. Naomi had never seen so many calendar-worthy men under one roof. Most were married, some with kids, but that didn't stop half the female staff from needing to wipe drool off their chins as the men passed by. Naomi had even heard several male staff members comment on the Quinn's good looks. The whole group was tall, muscled, and had what could only be described as charisma and sex appeal in buckets.

After talking to several, she also realized they were some of the most down-to-earth people on the planet. There should be more Quinns. Clearly, none of these men had been on a dating site. Or, if they had, they'd been swiped right off the market in a manner of seconds. Seeing them had reminded her just how pitiful her recent dates had been. It was probably good to know there were men like the Quinns out there. Somewhere. Even if the supply was dwindling.

"Good," Rita said. "Our golden boy woke up. He's strong as an ox and my money is on him making a fast recovery and an even speedier exit."

"Why does that make you frown?" Naomi asked, and then the reason dawned on her. "Never mind. Forget I asked that question. You want him to stick around."

"He's gorgeous and single," Rita said before making eyes at Naomi. "We don't exactly see much of that around here with men like him."

"What? Someone who works in law enforcement?" Naomi asked. A man with a dangerous job wasn't someone she could allow herself to get attached to.

"Doesn't bother me," Rita commented before seeming to realize the faux pax. It wouldn't either. She hadn't lost her first real love to the military and her father to his job as supervisor at Austin PD. One Naomi'd lost by age fifteen and the other had died a year ago while serving his country. The two of them had had big plans for their future after his service. All of which had gone up in smoke when she'd lost the love of her life. They'd been high school sweethearts who'd gone separate ways before reuniting two years ago on social media. Life could be insanely cruel when it wanted to be. It had given her back her first love and then almost immediately taken him away again. And it was probably the anniversary of his death that had her feeling so off balance and melancholy, not to mention the timing of the so-called gifts.

Naomi might want to pick the Marshal's brain about safety measures for the parking lot, but she would leave the dating aspect up to her co-workers.

"Health-wise, he's recovering, though?" Naomi decided it was best to steer the conversation back on track. "No red flags to watch out for?"

"Absolutely none," Rita said. "He's doing so well, in fact, I was about to ask if he wanted me to bring in margaritas for a nightcap when I get off work."

Naomi cracked a smile.

"Oh yeah, I'm sure Gwen would love that," Naomi said. The floor supervisor was well known for not putting up with any shenanigans.

Rita's gaze widened as she popped her chin and looked directly at something or someone over Naomi's shoulder.

"She's standing right behind me, isn't she?" Naomi asked, praying it wasn't true but fearing the worst. Why was it the worst always seemed to be the guarantee?

"Not *right* behind you but she is heading this way," Rita said.

Naomi breathed a sigh of relief as she reached up and absently fingered the familiar dog tags that hung on a chain around her neck.

"And she just turned," Rita said with an exhale. "We're safe."

"Who else came in today? Anyone I need to focus on or be concerned about?" Naomi asked, redirecting the conversation back to patients and her comfort zone.

"It was quiet aside from gorgeous in there. Since he arrived, it seems like every single nurse in the building has come up with an excuse to be on our floor," Rita said as she rolled her eyes. Her gaze dipped to the dog tags around Naomi's neck. Her work friend had tried to convince Naomi to stop wearing them, but it was all she had left of Gavin Rosemont. The second date she'd gone on from the app had commented on them too. He was history the minute he made a face after hearing who they belonged to. She'd left out the part about her and Gavin planning to get married, saying only that they were her high school sweetheart's.

Thinking about it, wearing her late fiancé's dog tags probably did make her seem hung up on the past. Was she? The short answer was yes.

The tingly feeling returned. Naomi glanced around as she half-listened to Rita's plans for her day off tomorrow.

"You should know the Marshal is the hospital's favorite patient," Rita continued after clearing her throat. She must have realized Naomi had zoned out.

"Why is that?" she asked. Hospital administration wouldn't care about his looks.

"I'm only saying it because you should probably stop in his room first," Rita said on a shrug. "I guess the family hands a lot of money out for charity and hospitals are at the top of their list."

"Good to know," Naomi said, figuring this patient's stay just became political for administration. "What about the family and visitation? Anything else I should know? Have they worked anything out that should be on my radar?"

"They have special permission to stay round the clock and the family members seem to have worked out shifts," Rita explained. "As a matter of fact, here comes one now."

A seriously good-looking man stepped into the hallway, gave a quick glance, and then headed toward the elevator bank.

"I should probably duck into the room while the patient is alone for a few seconds then," Naomi said as she smiled at the visitor.

"Good idea," Rita agreed.

Naomi hoped so. She'd thought about the patient in room 724 more than she cared to admit today.

CHAPTER TWO

If Harding Quinn had to sit in this bed much longer, he'd go stir crazy.

"Good evening. I'll be your nurse tonight." A tall auburn-haired beauty walked into the room and almost straight to the chalkboard opposite the bed. "My name is Naomi." She erased Rita's name and wrote hers. "I heard you had a good day."

When Naomi turned around to face him, his heart skipped a couple of beats. He blamed it on the painkillers and lack of exercise because heaven knew he was long out of high school. His suddenly sweaty palms begged to differ, so he cleared his throat in an attempt to regain his bearings and shake off this unexpected attraction to the night nurse.

"Did anyone mention when I might be released?" he asked.

"That's up to your doctor," Naomi said. She had the voice of one of his favorite country and western singers. It was the kind that seemed to settle on him and around him, giving him chills every time. Hot was too simple a word to describe Naomi's looks. She was the total package; long, lean legs that looked like they belonged to a professional dancer along with eyes that were as haunting as they were beautiful. Even from this distance he could see pain registered deep inside a slightly broken soul. The urge to put a smile on those full pink lips was a physical ache, which made no sense considering the two were strangers and he'd never felt this way before toward anyone.

"How soon will he or she stop by?" he continued, shaking off his initial reaction.

"I can check for you," she said, immediately turning toward the door.

"No. That's okay. I'm sure they'll be in when they make rounds," he said. Despite being a Quinn, he'd never been comfortable with special treatment and there was the simple fact he wanted her to stay. Harding had been brought up by the 'other' brother. The one who'd gone into law enforcement instead of cattle ranching. It was Harding's Uncle T.J. who had made the family a fortune. He'd split the mineral rights between all the boys, his seven sons and five nephews. Mineral rights were where the real money was despite his uncle starting and growing a successful cattle ranching business. All of Harding's cousins were home now, taking their rightful place on the ranch. Whereas, on Harding's side of the family, most worked in law enforcement. "The last time a doctor was here, I was out cold so I didn't get a chance to ask questions. My family filled me in as much as possible but they forgot to ask when I could get out of here."

The nurse nodded before walking over to his bedside and he was suddenly aware of how few clothes he had on. He almost laughed out loud at the thought he was worried about what he was wearing in a hospital. But, hey, these gowns left little to the imagination from behind and the opening in back wasn't a good look on anyone. Well, it might have looked good on her—but he stopped himself before his imagination could get carried away.

"Only the doctor can answer your question. Do you need anything else while I'm here? Anything to make you more comfortable?" she asked while checking the machines next to his bed.

"To be honest, this is all overkill," he said and then thought better of his word choice when she froze. "What I mean to say is that all these machines aren't necessary. I was barely grazed by a bullet and my family is already making too big a fuss over what happened."

"Just to be clear, 'what happened' was that you were shot in the line of duty. Is that correct?" she asked, her gaze lingering on him for a second longer than normal. The way she bit down on her bottom lip before turning back toward the sounds of the beeps had him wondering what question she'd wanted to ask.

"Yes, ma'am," he said, feeling a sudden chill in the air. "And now I need to get out of here, so I can rest at home."

"Where is that?" she asked after rolling her shoulders a couple of times. The movement was a sure sign she was stressed and he couldn't help but wonder what had happened. She couldn't be upset with him. They didn't know each other well enough for him to get under her skin this fast.

"Austin," he stated and caught the fact she bristled. "You don't like Austin?"

"Not particularly. There's way too much traffic for me," she said as she stared at his IV drip.

"I couldn't agree more there," he said. She made a good point. Traffic was a huge downside of living in the city.

A noise sounded in the hallway and Naomi practically jumped out of her skin. Her reaction was over the top, and made him wonder what had her on edge.

"Too much coffee?" he asked, his gaze settling on her hands—hands that were trembling.

"What? No," she said quickly. Too quickly.

"Then, do you mind if I ask what's going on?" he asked, figuring she might not tell him but at least he'd done his part to find out so he could offer assistance. Call it a job hazard but he had a difficult time ignoring someone when the person seemed like they were in trouble. Her body language indicated she was stressed. Could be work-related but his gut instincts honed by years of experience said this was personal.

"Someone I went on a date with recently seems to have developed feelings for me that I don't reciprocate," she said on a sharp sigh, surprising him with her honesty. As she turned to face him, the full force of her violet eyes on him caused the unfamiliar ache in his chest to return. Well, now he was becoming one of those 'poor me' country songs where an attraction was unrequited. This deep-in-the-chest feeling certainly couldn't be love after knowing Naomi for all of five minutes.

"Pardon the question, but have you told him straight out that he needs to move on? Some folks need a direct approach," he said, wondering how much more there was to the story.

"I would be happy to, if I knew who he was," she immediately countered. She seemed to hear how that sounded and he probably gave her quite the confused look because she added, "My co-worker talked me into signing up on one of those app things for dating." She absently fingered a set of dog tags on a chain around her neck. Did she realize she was doing it? "And I went on a few dates just to get it out of the way."

She flashed eyes at him as he quirked a brow.

"I probably sound like a terrible person right now," she said, and her cheeks turned five shades of red.

"There's nothing wrong with dating or those apps," he said, hoping the reassurance could make her feel a little better. She'd done the same thing millions of others had. Dating apps were nothing new and quite a few people found the loves of their lives on one. The part where she'd described dating as *getting it out of the way* caused questions to form in his mind.

"Really? Which one are you on?" she asked. There was more than a hint of curiosity in her eyes.

"Me?" he asked with complete shock in his voice. "None. But that doesn't mean I haven't considered it, with my strange hours and line of work. Most of the people I meet on the job end up in handcuffs." He hoped the joke would lighten the mood and help her feel less embarrassed.

Naomi's face broke into a smile. Mission accomplished. Though, he didn't want to think too hard about how much her smile warmed him.

"I guess being in law enforcement makes it hard to meet people," she said.

"Meeting people isn't the problem. Going on a date when you'd have to pick them up after they made bail is rough," he continued, laughing at his own joke. He winced. The pain was real and he'd refused to take much more than prescription-strength ibuprofen.

"Laughing is probably a bad idea when you have stitches above a bruised rib," she said with compassion in those violet hues.

"Just bruised?" he said on another laugh. "It should be broken with this much pain. Of course, that would take longer to heal so I don't wish that on myself."

"I'm sure the doctor will fill you in and I'm pretty sure I saw your brother in the hallway earlier. He'll be heading this way soon," she said, and he could tell based on her tone she was about to excuse herself. The odd thing about this conversation was that he didn't want it to end. "I should probably save him from Rita in case she intercepts him on his way back."

"Tell me more about the mystery guy," Harding said, circling back to their earlier thread. "What makes you think he isn't getting the hint?"

She hesitated for a long moment, shifting her weight from her left foot to her right in a sure sign she was considering what, if anything else, she should share. Then, she glanced at the door and seemed satisfied that they would be alone for a couple more minutes while Harding tried to sit up a little more. The hospital was no place to get rest and now that he'd sailed through surgery and was on the road to recovery, he needed to figure out how to get the doctor to sign off on release papers so he could get out of here.

"There have been 'presents' left on my car, which probably sounds like I'm being paranoid, but a dead rose didn't sit well," she said. Those last words seemed to rush out of her mouth like she was making an apology for being freaked out.

"I always tell people to listen to their instincts in these circumstances," he reassured.

"Really?" She seemed genuinely caught off guard by his answer.

"Yes," he said. "That little warning voice in the back of your mind is usually right. And there's no harm done on the rare occasion it's wrong."

"Other than being embarrassed," she said quietly.

"Better embarrassed than the alternative," he pointed out. "I'm not trying to scare you in saying that by any means. It's just that I have a lot of experience dealing with people who ignored their intuition and in hindsight they have a whole lot of regret. Plus, I agree. A dead rose is unusual. How dead was it? As in, did he buy it and forget to keep it watered before he could get it to you? Or, was being dead the point?"

"I'd say the latter." She started fingering the embossed letters on the dog tags again and he wondered if she realized she was doing it. Clearly, the tags belonged to someone she cared about and was very close to. The fact she wore them revealed something terrible had happened to their owner. It was a stark reminder of the dangers of certain jobs—jobs like his.

"Then, you have a right to be concerned," he confirmed.

"You know, one of my tires was low on air the day he left me the rose. I never really connected the dots before now. It seemed random because there was no nail or slit in the tire. Someone had just let the air out. Since the tire was fairly new, I thought I got a leaky one but the place where I bought it denied there was a problem," she said.

"That's exactly what I'm talking about. Small events, which at the time don't seem like anything to worry about, surrounding a big event aren't missed by our brains. We dismiss them but the signs are often there," he said.

Naomi nodded and he could almost see the wheels turning in her mind.

"There was no note with either the rose or the teddy bear, and the bear had a small stain on it that I thought might have been from a marker of some kind, or that maybe the guy had been eating fast food," she said.

"Fast food?" he asked.

"Ketchup," she clarified. "In the moment, I had this thought of, like, what if this is blood. I had no idea where the notion came from, so I dismissed it immediately."

Blood? Now Harding's danger antenna was up.

CHAPTER THREE

Icy fingers gripped Naomi's spine as she recounted recent events and her initial reactions to each one with Harding Quinn.

"How long ago did this start and how much time passed in between gifts?" Harding asked. He shifted in the bed and it was easy to see that he was having a difficult time getting comfortable.

A light tap at the door was followed by Dr. Juno's voice. "Hello."

"Come in, Dr. Juno," Naomi said, straightening up after being in what had felt like an intimate conversation with Harding. Strange because she was at work and had never experienced a feeling of intimacy while speaking to a patient before. She shot a quick apology toward Harding for overstaying her welcome. "I was on my way out."

"Can you come back?" he asked in barely a whisper. "I'd like to finish this conversation and offer some advice."

She gave a slight nod as the doctor entered the room and then moved to the foot of the bed.

Dr. Juno was in stark contrast to the man in the bed. Jeffrey Juno had all black hair, a slight frame, and wore thick-rimmed glasses that created a bug-eye effect. He shuffled in as Naomi took a couple of steps away from the bed. She wasn't sure why she suddenly felt the need to make sure the doctor knew she wasn't getting too close to a patient. More of that instinct kicking in that said the doctor wouldn't approve of her sharing her personal situation with his patient? Or was it the fact she felt like she'd violated a hospital policy by engaging in what had felt like an intimate conversation with Harding?

It wasn't, though, she reminded herself.

"Since you're on shift tonight, you might as well stick around and hear the patient's questions," Dr. Juno said to her. He'd asked her to call him Jeffrey six months ago when he first started but it had never felt right.

"Thank you, Doctor," she said, folding her arms and preparing to listen closely for instructions.

"My name is Dr. Juno." He offered a handshake to Harding, who took it. The latter man's hand dwarfed the doctor's.

Naomi moved to the chalkboard before erasing the dayshift doc's name. She wrote *Dr. Juno* in place directly above hers. There was a distinct hierarchy in the medical field, and she was reminded of it every time she walked into a patient's room and glanced at the blackboard.

"Harding Quinn," he said after the pair shook hands.

Dr. Juno had the patient's chart tucked underneath

his left arm. He pulled it out, opened it, and glanced at the pages. After nodding his head a couple of times, he lifted his gaze to meet Harding's, who had been studying the doctor.

"Level with me," Harding began, and Naomi immediately saw where this was going. "How soon can I get out of here?"

Yes, that was exactly what she thought his question would be.

"Surgery went well. You'll be receiving a visit from Dr. Stuber soon to answer any questions there," Dr. Juno said. He pushed his glasses up his nose with his index finger. "Getting out of here is a bit more complicated."

"Even if I'll sleep better at home?" Harding asked.

Naomi had never encountered a law enforcement officer or firefighter who wanted to stick around in a hospital a second longer than absolutely necessary. She had to admit that she admired men and women who ran toward danger rather than from it, and she had all the respect in the world for them. But after losing her father, and then Gavin, she would hold all that admiration from a distance. Harding had been lucky this time. If the shooter had aimed a little more to the left, he would have been struck in the heart.

"It's too early to talk about releasing you," Dr. Juno began. "Especially under these circumstances."

"What circumstances?" Harding asked. He'd locked onto the possibility faster than most folks who came through. His impatience rolled off him in palpable waves and she half feared he would rip out his own IV so he could walk out of there.

"Single. You do live alone, don't you?" Dr. Juno asked.

"Yes, but—"

"So there's no one to make certain you have food and hydrate or to check that you're healing properly." Dr. Juno's self-satisfied grin was probably too early for a battle with someone like Harding Quinn.

Naomi didn't want to admit the summersaults happening in her stomach at the realization Harding was single. Who wouldn't be attracted to him with that carved from granite jawline? A hawk-like nose wasn't normally so attractive on a man, but it gave Harding an edgy look. Full, thick lips softened a face of hard angles and planes and made her wonder for half a second what they might feel like feathering kisses down her neck.

Of course she was attracted to Harding Quinn. Her and the rest of the floor. Heck, probably the entire hospital staff too. When someone with his good looks showed up, the gossip mill seemed to light up. Since his family had stopped by and were still filing in, there was no doubt word had gotten around about the gorgeous as sin Marshal.

Speaking of family, a man who looked enough like Harding to realize the two were related came walking into the room. One glance at the doctor and the guy hid a sack of something that smelled amazing behind his back. It didn't take long to realize what he was hiding. Despite the artful move, Dr. Juno wrinkled his nose in disapproval. There was no disguising the smell of burgers from B.J.'s.

"I can come back," the tall, handsome man said.

"Don't be ridiculous, Barrett," Harding said, wincing

as he moved. "Come on in and bring me supper."

"I'm afraid that's not permitted," Dr. Juno said with a frown.

"Can I ask you a question, Doctor?" Harding started as the guy he called Barrett began a slow smile.

"Yes. Of course." Dr. Juno didn't seem to realize it yet, but he was out of his league with this fast talker.

"What harm will a decent hamburger do?" he started and then put his hand up. "Before you answer that. Let me ask you this. Is it good for me to get a decent meal down?"

"Yes, it is," Dr. Juno responded as worry lines wrinkled his forehead. He was in his mid-forties and single. At least Naomi believed so. The man never wore a ring or spoke of a wife. A nurse on the third floor said he'd asked her out once. Naomi had overheard the pediatric floor nurse recounting the story to one of her friends in a hushed tone. There was something about the way Dr. Juno would suddenly be standing right behind someone like he'd appeared out of thin air that gave everyone the creeps.

With the return of Barrett to the room, Naomi figured the conversation about her secret admirer was most likely over. She needed to excuse herself and make rounds before Dr. Juno asked her about other patients. As it was, she'd been on duty for almost half an hour at this point and was still in the first patient's room. She'd intended to get in and out earlier. And yet the funny part was that she didn't want to leave. She wanted to stick around and get more advice from the Marshal while she had his attention. Besides, she didn't get the chance to answer his question. Too late now.

"I work out religiously and eat well when I'm not holed up in a hospital room. Since you won't let me leave, at least allow me the pleasure of a burger." Harding was convincing. One look at his body with muscles for days and it was easy to see that he wasn't lying about working out. The man's body looked like a temple of fitness. Naomi sighed quietly as she made a move for the door.

"I see that you're not taking all your pain medication," Dr. Juno continued.

"I'd rather listen to what my body is telling me," Harding stated.

Naomi smiled at that remark. He might be the most stubborn man she'd seen in a long time, but he was also right and seemed to know what he could handle.

"I'm not agreeing to let you eat outside food," Dr. Juno said on a defeated sigh. "But when I leave this room, I won't know what's happening. Will I?"

At least the defensive tone was out of Dr. Juno's voice.

Naomi could almost feel Harding smile from across the room and with her back to him.

"Does this mean you'll stay without me needing to request restraints?" Dr. Juno asked as he moved toward the door.

"No restraints necessary," Harding said. "In fact, I promise you'll be one of the first to know before I walk out that door."

The comment seemed to catch Dr. Juno off guard. He bristled but kept walking until he passed right by Naomi and entered the hallway. She gripped the door handle figuring she'd give Harding and Barrett a little privacy.

Once in the hallway, she exhaled and closed the door. Almost the second the snick sounded, the door swung open again nearly smacking her in the face. Startled, she jumped back a step just in time to miss a bloody nose.

"Sorry," Barrett said with a shocked look. He had the same sandy-blond hair as Harding and the two had enough similar features for anyone to see they were related. In her opinion, Harding was the better looking of the pair.

"It's fine," she said as she tried to calm her racing pulse. "No harm. I got out of the way in time."

"I didn't realize you'd be standing there," he continued, looking horrified that he came so close to nailing her.

"It's okay. Really," she said. "Did you need something?"

"My brother asked if you'd stop by when you got a chance," Barrett said. "He was cryptic about the reason but said you needed an answer about something, and he wanted a minute to think on it."

"Tell him that I figured it out, so not to worry," she said, figuring she'd taken up enough of the man's time.

"I will, but he'll be disappointed," Barrett said before thanking her for her time and then closing the door.

Naomi spent the next half hour on rounds. She kept glancing at Harding's door after taking her spot at the nurse's station to update the computer. The elevator bank was close enough to the nurse's station for her to see who came and went on the floor. Sara came rushing toward the station, clutching the strap of her purse. Head down, she walked right past Naomi and straight to the cabinets in back where they locked up their handbags before signing in on the computer to note their start time.

Sara rushed over, keeping her gaze trained on the white tile flooring.

"Did she notice how late I am?" Sara asked.

"I haven't talked to her yet," Naomi offered. Her heart went out to Sara because she always seemed a bundle of nerves. She would show up covering bruises on her arms and had covered up black eyes with makeup more than once. Rita had warned Naomi not to ask questions about Sara's home life. There was something about a teenage stepson and possibly an abusive husband.

Minding her own business was difficult when Naomi wanted to offer help.

Sara blew out a breath. The blonde nurse was in her late thirties and always smelled fresh from a smoke break. Patients complained from time to time. Sara had gotten a little bit better about it until today. The woman reeked of cigarettes.

"I have a rose-scented spritzer in my purse if you want to borrow it," Naomi offered, figuring Sara should know.

"Oh. Yeah. Sure. That would be great," Sara said, her voice raspy. There'd been a few questions raised about patients on the floor being charged for painkillers they swore they didn't take. It was difficult terrain to navigate as a nurse because the people scrutinizing their hospital bill had most likely been on strong pain relief during their stay. It was difficult to trust the judgment of someone who'd been on medication. She knew one hundred percent that she'd given a patient a painkiller only to have said patient hit the buzzer and demand her pills twenty minutes later. It was an honest mistake, but a complaint the hospital took seriously since that time Ivy Edwards had been pocketing pills that her patients refused to take.

Naomi made a note to keep an eye on Harding's file since he was refusing some of his medication. She would make sure the pills weren't ending up in Sara's pocket and then going home with her. Naomi hated to think about a co-worker that way but Rita had warned Naomi about the possibility with Sara, and now the information was stuck inside Naomi's brain.

Since the Marshal had requested Naomi come back, she figured she could ask him about it then. She retrieved her spritzer and handed the bottle over to Sara.

"I'll take number 724," Sara said. She had extra concealer underneath her left eye. Was she hiding another black eye? Naomi's heart dropped and she wished there was something she could say that might help despite Sara being prickly toward her.

"I've already been in and for some reason he asked to see me. You can have him tomorrow night if you want," Naomi said, half expecting an argument.

"Fine." Sara shrugged. It was shaping up to be a long shift. Working with Sara had never been Naomi's favorite but they generally stayed out of each other's way. They kept a cordial working relationship. But then,

Naomi had never really seen Sara buddy up to anyone at work. The thought struck Naomi as strange considering they worked twelve-hour shifts together.

Hope Rawlins zoomed past the desk.

"Hey ladies," Hope said as she breezed on by. She had a full head of gray hair and one strand of purple. Despite being in her early fifties, she could run circles around nurses half her age.

"Morning, Hope," Naomi said with a smile.

"It is for us," Hope said, returning the smile as she referred to the three of them working the overnight shift. Their days and nights were flipped, which Naomi preferred after losing Gavin. Facing going to an empty bed at night had been too much. This way, when they would have curled up to watch a movie when he was home, she was getting ready for work. No more long nights lying awake, staring at the ceiling. Having an entirely different schedule, a new routine had saved her.

"Guess I'll take odd-numbered rooms then," Sara said after pumping a couple of squirts. She handed over the bottle with a curt *thank you*.

Hope was a floater, covering three floors and going where she was needed. Too bad Sara wasn't the floater tonight, was all Naomi could think.

"Sounds good," Naomi agreed. There weren't enough patients to keep two nurses busy, so this was probably going to be a long night. At this point, all she could do to rally her spirits was think about having the next three days off work. Feet up, she intended to watch old movies and drink too much tea.

Sara disappeared down the hallway. Naomi wished she knew her co-worker well enough to ask questions about her personal life. When she thought about what Harding Quinn had said about trusting her intuition, she worried for Sara.

The door to room number 724 opened and, speaking of the handsome devil, out came Harding.

———

"What are you doing out of bed?" Naomi asked Harding as he hobbled out of his room. Frustration about being shot in the first place stung his pride. The hospital gown gave him another punch. Now that he was out of surgery and on the road to recovery, he needed out of this place.

"Finding out who I need to speak to in order to authorize my release," he said with determination.

"Dr. Juno all but agreed to let you eat the hamburger. Are you trying to get me in trouble?" she scowled, coming around the nurse's station as she urged him back a couple of steps.

Barrett sidestepped Harding, moving into the hallway.

"I've been trying to tell my brother that leaving is a bad idea," Barrett said. "But a bull doesn't have anything on him in the stubborn department once he digs his heels in."

"Perhaps I should up his dosage to get him on his backside for the night," Naomi said to Barrett like Harding wasn't standing right there.

Before he could work up a good argument, her face broke into a wide smile.

"Not funny," he countered.

"I can see how someone in your line of work would view being stuck in a hospital bed as just about the worst thing that could happen to a person," she said in a surprising show of understanding. "You're our first U.S. Marshal but we've had other lawmen and firefighters come through. Believe me when I say none of them wanted to stick around."

"How did they get out?" Harding asked. He'd wrapped a blanket around himself as he grabbed onto the IV cart, dragging it behind him. It was meant for him to be able to get up and go to the bathroom by himself, but he intended to march out of there as soon as he got the green light. Leaving beforehand would be frowned on by the department.

"It might surprise you to learn they actually stayed," she said, taking a step toward him.

He instinctively took another step back out of politeness and almost chuckled. She was good at her job, which seemed to include wrangling cranky patients.

"How was your burger, by the way?" she asked in an obvious attempt to distract him.

"Good," he said, going along with it.

"You asked me to stop by later. Is now a good time?" She folded her arms across her chest, fortifying herself for a negative response.

"I guess so," he said. "If you promise to talk about my release as part of the deal."

"Done," she said before nodding to Barrett. "There's a gas station down the street that brews the absolute best cup of coffee. Mind going out for it?"

"I guess not." He really chuckled.

"You already know I take mine black," Harding said,

figuring they could finally get down to business and he could be home in the next couple of hours. The caffeine should last just long enough to get him tucked into his own bed.

"The coffee is for me," Naomi said, not backing down or taking her gaze from Harding.

He had to admit to being amused. And he could further admit he wanted to witness her tactic to getting him to agree to stay overnight. People didn't usually surprise him. She did and he was intrigued by her.

"Yes, ma'am," Barrett said with a smile. "I believe I know just where you're talking about. Had a cup from there on my way in."

Naomi turned as he walked past her and mouthed something Harding couldn't hear. Barrett saluted and then headed down the hallway.

"After you," Harding said, stepping aside and waving his hand like he was presenting the way into his room.

"Thank you," she said rather pristine for someone who'd just ordered someone three times her physical size to a gas station for a midnight coffee run.

Harding followed Naomi inside the room before taking one of the empty seats.

"You look a little pale if you don't mind my saying so." She studied him. "I can help you get back in bed if you'd like."

"I'm fine. Sitting up will help stave off some of the nausea," he admitted.

"I have something that can help with that if you're game," she said, reaching into the pouch of her pale blue uniform.

"Sure, why not," he said.

She handed over a packet. "Pop it open and put it on your tongue," she instructed.

He did and she almost seemed surprised he didn't put up an argument. A few seconds later, his stomach eased.

"Thank you," he said, conceding that she was right.

"I have a few tricks up my sleeve that can help," she said with a self-satisfied smile.

"Remind me of the fact the next time I feel sick," he said. Then again, he didn't plan to be around long enough. "So, why are they really keeping me here?"

"Honestly," she started, leaning forward in a conspiratorial tone, "most likely for observation. You're young, healthy, and strong." Her cheeks turned red as she said those last words. "Which is only to say that you're going to be fine. It's normal to keep someone a couple of days just to make sure nothing goes wrong after surgery."

"So, what I'm hearing is that it's safe for me to walk out of here right now," he said.

"Probably," she admitted. "But can I ask a question?"

"Shoot," he said, regretting his word choice almost the minute it left his mouth. In fact, he'd been shot at plenty of times during his time at the U.S. Marshals Service. Normally, he knew when to duck.

"What's the rush?" Naomi asked. "Is there someone at home you need to get back to?"

"No," Harding admitted. He'd never had a problem admitting to a lack of a dating life before. Why did it suddenly embarrass him now? "I'd like to be in my own clothes, and it'd be great if I wasn't hooked up to something that beeped every few seconds."

She stood up and moved over to the machines

before playing around with a couple of nobs. The noises weakened until they were barely audible.

"I'm not supposed to do this, so you didn't see me," she said.

"I didn't even see your ghost," he said with a smile. "And thank you."

"You're welcome. What else can I for you?" she asked, then quickly added, "besides drive the getaway car?"

Harding laughed. He liked her sense of humor and figured she would need one working with cranky patients like him all day.

"Tell me more about your situation," he said as he held up a hand. "I'm not trying to pry but I'd prefer to keep my mind busy. Work has always done that for me and we got interrupted before you had a chance to answer my question earlier."

"I have a puzzle book if you'd like to use it to relax," she offered.

"No, thanks. I'd rather hear more about you," he stated.

"What can I say?" she said on a non-comital shrug. She stood there, quiet, and he picked up on a moment of hesitation. "I heard what you said earlier and now a few other things are clicking into place."

"You were talking about a teddy bear," he said, and I believe I asked if you still have it. It's not too late to run forensics on it."

"Now I wish I'd kept it just for that reason," she said. "It creeped me out, so I dropped it in the dumpster at work. It's long gone by now and probably destroyed at the dump."

"Next time, save everything and try not to get your fingerprints on any evidence," he said, wishing he could examine the evidence.

"You think this might be that serious?" she asked as a tremor rocked her body.

"I do," he stated. "I'm always going to err on the side of caution, though. Plus, when someone gets away with something like this, they often escalate. Maybe not with you. Or maybe they do. Depends on whether or not he's become fixated."

"I don't like the sound of that," she said, rubbing her arms like she was trying to stave off a sudden chill.

"I'd advise you to stick with the buddy system for a few weeks at a minimum. Although, since you come in at night when it's dark, I'd advise you to park near a light or as close to the building as possible," he stated.

"I always park as close to the ER doors as possible. Lighting in the parking lot overall is terrible, but I can get some activity there once in a while at least," she said.

"What about administration? Have you complained to them about the problem? I'm sure if you grabbed a couple of your friends and brought them to the meeting they would have to listen. That, or at the very least get a complaint on record. You'd be surprised at how quickly folks start acting when documentation becomes involved," he stated.

Naomi nodded her head.

"I brought the issue up with Rod, head of security," she said. "But that's a good point about rallying the other nurses."

"And?"

"He basically made it seem like we live in an area where there's no crime and that I was being 'silly' bringing up my concerns about 'gifts' being left on my vehicle at work," she said.

Harding grunted. "You have to be kidding me," he said.

"I wish," she stated.

"Before I leave, I'll request a meeting with him. Someone claiming to be head of security needs to take people's complaints more seriously," he ground out. The man was unbelievable, and a disgrace to the field with that attitude. "Good lighting should be a basic fact of every workplace when employees come and go at all hours."

"He said more women are abducted from the grocery store parking lot in broad daylight than from hospital parking lots at any time night or day," she continued.

"Now, I really need to speak to this jerk," Harding said.

A small smile upturned the corners of Naomi's pink lips at his disgust for Rod. Maybe he scored a little bit of her trust along the way.

"Sorry about getting rid of your brother," she said.

"Why?" he asked.

"I thought you might be easier to sway if he wasn't in the room," she admitted with a sneaky smile.

Well, now Harding really did laugh. It hurt. It also endeared this stranger to him in a way he didn't want or need. And he needed to figure out how he felt about that before he walked out of this hospital and out of her life.

CHAPTER FOUR

"Give me your best shot," Harding said. The grin on his face made Naomi rest a little easier, considering she'd gambled on the fact he had a sense of humor.

"What can it hurt to stay the night? My shift is over at eleven tomorrow morning and you'll be sleeping most of that time anyway if you know what's good for you," Naomi said by way of plea bargain.

He shot her a look that said they both knew he wouldn't get a wink in this place, so she put her hands up, palms out in the surrender position.

"You got me there," she said. "You probably won't sleep but let's not forget you have refused most of the pain medications in favor of ibuprofen, so you'll probably have the same result at home."

"Fair point," he conceded. "Here's the other thing, my family will worry about me a whole lot less once I'm out of here and they are about to smother me as is. I don't know how much more of this attention I can take."

"I'll give you that one," she said. "I heard they pretty much lined the halls while you were on the surgical floor."

"They did and they have shifts worked out to come here while I'm in the hospital," he stated, rolling his eyes in the process.

"Not everyone has a family who cares whether they live or die, so some people might consider themselves fortunate to have so much concern," she pointed out without giving away anything about her personal situation. Or at least she believed she wasn't when she said the words. His reaction happened in a blink, but an emotion passed behind his eyes that told her how much he understood why she might say those words. So much for being secretive.

"That's true," he said like he was choosing his next words carefully. "Families can be amazing things. They can also be hurtful things and things that make us feel like we're not quite enough in just being ourselves."

She sat there for a long moment, letting those words sink in.

It didn't take long to realize she'd fallen into the trap of thinking the grass was always greener on the other side.

"I guess there's good and bad to every situation," she admitted.

"There is," he said. "Don't get me wrong, I love my big family. My brothers are everything to me and I grew up close to my cousins, as well. I wouldn't have my life any other way. I did, however, grow up around a whole lot of testosterone and very little estrogen. It has made my job harder in some ways, especially in the early days.

I didn't always know what to say or how to handle a delicate situation. I'd like to think I've gotten better with age and experience, but who knows."

"Sounds like you try to get it right, so I'm sure you're doing better than you think," she said by way of encouragement. She doubted Harding even noticed but when he was the slightest bit unsure of himself, his right eyebrow twitched just the slightest.

"I appreciate your confidence," he said with an honesty that caused her chest to squeeze. There should be more men like Harding Quinn in the world. It would be a much better place and a whole lot easier to find someone to date as long as they didn't work in a dangerous job.

"Just making an observation," she said and could feel her cheeks flame. They didn't have a whole lot of time before his brother returned, so she wanted to ask his advice. "And speaking of which, what do you think I should do next about my current situation? I've already made a note to grab a couple of nurses and take the lighting request to management. What else can I do? Anything to make the gifts stop?"

"That's tricky," he said. "Maybe we could make a list of possible suspects. See if any of the names pop out. Then, we have to think about opportunity. Who would have access to your vehicle? That kind of information can be helpful."

"Sadly, pretty much everyone has access out in the parking lot. I drive something distinct too. It's not exactly brand new. The handful of dates I had from the app before I disabled it would all know my vehicle if they watched me pull up to the meeting place," she said.

Talking about her dating life with Harding made her uncomfortable. He was a professional and she was asking for his advice. This should be a straightforward exchange. So, it caught her off guard that she felt oddly protective over talking about past dates with him, as though the two were on a date themselves.

"Okay, let's start by making a list of names," he said. "Throw out the names of individuals you went out with…" He glanced around like he was looking for something to write with.

"Hold on," she said before dashing out to the nurse's station. Sara passed by and shot a disapproving look as Naomi hustled back into Harding's room. She didn't have time to explain to Sara that he was helping figure out who might be leaving disturbing gifts—gifts Sara had no idea were being left in the first place. Explaining would require a whole conversation with a co-worker Naomi didn't feel close to. If she thought anyone else might be in danger, that would be a different story.

Harding nodded his approval when he saw the pad of paper and pen in her hand. She took a seat opposite him and leaned forward with the pad resting on her thigh.

"Write down the names of your dates and when the two of you went out. Capture everything you remember, like where you went and what time," he said, and she thought she saw an emotion flashed behind his eyes that looked a lot of jealousy. Which was too bizarre and probably a figment of her imagination. Considering she'd only known this man a couple of hours at this point, she decided not to put too much stock in what she believed she saw.

"One question," she said. "How do I know if they gave me their real name? The site didn't exactly do a background check on me."

"That's a good question actually. Write down the name they gave you and their screen name if you remember it," he said. "We can re-sign up for the site if need be or contact someone in their home office to do a little digging into backgrounds."

"Okay," she said, writing down the five names she remembered. "This site only gives first names and it's up to the females to swipe. At that point, we share what we're comfortable with. My friend who convinced me to sign up for the app said it's the best way for a woman to be in control. That was the point of this one and why she likes it."

"Who is this friend and is she on the app?" he asked.

"Rita is her name and she was your nurse today," she said.

"I remember her," he said with a look that said Rita had spent more time in his room than was probably necessary. She'd made no secret out of thinking the man was gorgeous and wishing she could date him, one of his brothers, or any one of his cousins. Of course, Rita had been quick to notice and mention that many of the Quinn men were already spoken for.

"Sorry," she said by way of apology for her friend's behavior.

"It's not a problem," he said on a laugh. It was then she realized a guy as gorgeous as Harding most likely had a long list of people he spent time with, since he'd already said there was no one special at home. Not having a partner didn't mean no dating.

"She can be a bit much, but she has a heart of gold and would do anything for a friend," she stated before realizing she might have oversold her buddy. "Did that come off as defensive?"

"A little," he said with a grin. "But you sound like a good friend, and that's more important."

"Rita is one of the few people I get along with and trust," she admitted, unsure of why she was suddenly so comfortable spilling her secrets to a near stranger. Or maybe that was the easy part. Talking to someone she didn't know from Adam and who would walk, or in his case be wheeled, out the door most likely before her next shift in three days never to be seen again. Wasn't that the reason folks said they went on talk shows and spilled their innermost secrets? Because it was somehow easier than speaking directly to the one person they probably should have a conversation with?

Theo stepped inside the room. He took two steps inside and held tightly to a broom. "I noticed you weren't at the nurse's station for a l-l-long time. Are y-y-y-ou okay?"

"Me?" she asked. "Of course, Theo. I'm talking to a patient right now, but do you need something?"

He tightened and released his grip on the broom handle a couple of times before speaking without making eye contact.

"No. I guess not," he finally said but he didn't look ready to walk out the door.

What was that all about?

"I-I-I just heard r-rumors and I thought I should make sure you're okay if you stay in a patient's room too long," Theo explained.

"Well, thank you," she said. "But you really don't have to worry about me." The comment about rumors didn't sit well. "What have you heard that would make you think you need to check up on me?"

"Not you," he said. "Them." He nodded toward Harding as though he was oblivious to what was happening.

"Oh, okay," she continued. "I'm good, so you can keep on working as you were."

"All right. D-d-do you want my phone number?" Theo continued.

"No, thank you," she said. "Besides, I already have it. Remember? I'll be fine, but I do need to get back to work."

Barrett picked that moment to return with coffee. Theo turned and almost bumped into the much taller man. In fact, Barrett took up the entire doorway much in the same way Harding had moments ago. At this point, she was beginning to believe trying to get advice from him was a lost cause.

"Excuse me," Theo said, puffing his chest out in an aggressive move she'd never seen before.

Thankfully, Barrett smiled and sidestepped Theo, who immediately disappeared into the hallway.

"Do I want to ask what that was about?" Barrett handed over the coffee and retained one for himself.

"I think my co-worker decided to be protective over me," she said.

Harding's eyebrow shot up. "Is that something he's done before?" he asked.

"Not really. He barely ever speaks to me and almost always keeps his gaze to the floor as though he's afraid I might bite if we happen to be in the same elevator together," she admitted. The raised eyebrow had her concerned. She also needed to circle back to ask Theo what he meant about the rumors. "But then, he's like that with everyone so this is out of character."

"Put his name on the list," Harding said, and her stomach dropped.

CHAPTER FIVE

Harding had seen more in his tenure at the U.S. Marshals Service than anyone probably should in one lifetime. When a woman was being harassed, it was most often by someone she knew fairly well instead of a stranger or one-off date. He wouldn't rule anything out at this point, but Theo needed to go on the list.

"Are you sure?" she asked as she placed a hand over her mouth. "I mean, he's very innocent. I think his mother still packs his lunches, despite him celebrating his thirtieth birthday recently."

"Does she drive him to and from work?" Harding asked, putting on his investigator hat after giving Barrett a quick high level of the situation.

"I think he takes the bus and walks the two blocks," she said.

"Then, he could have access to your vehicle. Since the incidences happen at work, this is the first place to start looking," Barrett interjected as Harding nodded.

"I was just about to say the same thing," he said.

"Makes sense. The people I dated didn't have my home address. I was...*am*...private about that," she informed.

"You mentioned that you're not on the app any longer," he said. "Did the bad dates turn you off?"

He studied her as she absently fingered the dog tags around her neck, and he wanted to know if the owner was the real reason.

"I'm not, and yes to an extent," she admitted. She shot a glance at Barrett, thanked him for the coffee, and then said, "dating isn't for me right now."

Based on her answer, he surmised that she was still hung up on the owner of those tags. A dating app that she'd basically been pushed by a friend to join would signal that her friend believed enough time had passed between being in a relationship with Dog Tags and now, and that Naomi should move on. The fact she followed through the with app and a couple of dates told him that she wanted to be ready to move on, or maybe just stop being in pain, but couldn't let go. Basically, the auburn beauty was off limits, which wasn't a problem for him.

In fact, it might just work to his advantage because he had a proposition for her and neither needed the complication of being tempted to act on an attraction.

Since the doctor didn't want to release Harding because he didn't have anyone at home to care for him, he needed to hire a nurse. Who better than someone who worked at the very hospital he was being released from?

"Can I ask a question about your schedule?" Harding asked.

She blinked a couple of times, clearly surprised by the change in direction of the conversation.

"Sure," she finally said. "I mean, if I can't trust a U.S. Marshal with personal information, who can I?"

He smiled.

"Rita mentioned that she wished she had tomorrow off and she told me about the kinds of shifts you work," he hedged. "I'm pretty sure she mentioned something about me not getting too attached to the night nurse since this was your last shift this week."

"Did she really?" Naomi asked with a playful look in her eyes. "Sounds about right."

"And I thought you mentioned being off for a few days after tonight. Are you? Off the next few days?" he continued, realizing he probably sounded like an investigator rather than a patient.

"Yes, I am. After tonight, I'm off for three days, but I don't see how that—"

"What's the possibility of hiring you for home care?" he asked. "I'd make it worth your while financially."

"Believe it or not, I use my days off to rest so I can come back here and be on my feet twelve hours a day. Without that period of rest, I'd be useless to my patients," she explained but she spoke with very little conviction and he wondered if there wasn't something else bothering her about the offer.

He decided to sweeten the pot and see what she thought.

"I have no problem paying you, and one patient in his home environment who is self-sufficient shouldn't wear you out too much," he reasoned. "And the bonus is that you'd get unfettered access to a law enforcement official. I can help you sort out the issue you've been having and you won't have to send anyone out for coffee to speak to me privately because the coffee at my house is just fine. What do you think?"

"It's a great offer, but I'd better get back to work," she stated as she practically bolted toward the door.

Barrett stood at the window, looking out at the blackness.

Well, he'd done it now. He'd run her off before he could secure her help. In fact, he couldn't remember the last time someone had needed to get away from him so fast and that was saying a whole lot considering his profession.

"Tell me what's going on with the nurse," Barrett said. It was then Harding realized his brother had been studying him from across the room.

"Nothing. Why? What do you think is happening?" Harding asked a little too quickly, and he could hear the defensiveness in his own voice. He muttered a curse with the full knowledge he wasn't normally one to show his hand.

The corners of Barrett's lips upturned in a grin.

"Not a thing," his brother said, hand up and one palm out in the surrender position.

"Naomi asked for my advice about the potential stalker situation," Harding said, work talk would be the best distraction.

"Can you share more details?" Barrett took a sip of his coffee while waiting for a response.

Harding filled his brother in. Considering Barrett also worked for the U.S. Marshals Service, his perspective would be golden in a situation like Naomi's.

"I agree about creating the suspect list," Barrett said, nodding. He stood up, walked to the window, and then set his coffee on the sill. "The gifts came in order, when you really think about it. What does a guy bring on a date?"

"Flowers, for one," Harding said.

"Some folks bring a gift next, and a teddy bear seems like a decision about personal taste," Barrett said. "Probably more common on Valentine's Day with the obligatory box of chocolates. And, I'm also thinking high school unless the gift was specifically asked for."

"Agreed," Harding stated. "I'd even extend the bear to college, as some young people would see it as a cute gesture."

"I could see that," Barrett agreed.

"I agree with your assessment of it being a personal thing. It's not something many would show up with unless they were certain the intended would want one," Harding said.

"Right," Barrett agreed.

"Naomi seemed good with all my ideas, until I told her to put Theo on the suspect list," Harding said.

"He does seem innocent and harmless," Barrett said before adding, "at least on the surface."

"The teddy bear would make sense coming from someone like him," Harding said. "It was also obvious he has a crush on her."

"I would agree with you there," Barrett said. "Most guys who are smaller in stature than me make a strong attempt to get out of my way. He seemed to have a bone to pick with me earlier when I walked into your room. At the time, it came out of the blue."

"I thought so too," Harding said. "He wasn't exactly subtle." And then it dawned on Harding why Naomi might have needed to get out of the room. "He mentioned a rumor had already started going around the hospital that Naomi was spending too much time in here."

"Doesn't sound good for a nurse's career to be seen staying too long in a single guy's room," Barrett reasoned. "I'm sure a small hospital can be a bit like living in a small town. Word travels fast."

"And rumors can ruin a reputation if left unchecked," Harding said, thinking he really was caught between a rock and a hard place with Naomi. Asking her to come back inside his room might put her career in jeopardy. If he went into the hallway to speak to her, it might draw even more attention to the situation.

A knock at the door came a few seconds before it opened and a new nurse walked inside.

"Hi, my name is Sara. There's been a change of plans tonight. I'll be your nurse," the blonde said as she went straight to the chalkboard and erased Naomi's name.

"Okay. Thanks for letting me know," Harding said, figuring that putting up a fight would only make matters worse even though his chest deflated with the change of plans. Apparently, Naomi being in his room for as long as she was earlier had put her in an incriminating light with the hospital.

Barrett slid a look in Harding's direction that said his brother was thinking along the same lines. They knew each other well enough to read an expression without needing to speak the words outright.

"My pleasure," Sara said, and the words sounded a

little too happy for the situation, almost like she'd won a bet.

"I'm good right now but I know where the button is if that changes," Harding said, motioning toward the call button attached to the armrest.

"Okay, sounds good." With that, Sara exited the room.

The minute the door closed, Barrett issued a disgruntled grunt.

"Isn't that convenient," he said.

"Now, I'm wondering if this stalking case is a date fixation or something else," Harding said. "Like plain old harassment."

A whole lot of questions surfaced now. He wondered if Naomi had made any enemies at work. The gossip mill could be cruel when it wanted to be. Was there more to it than talk? Did someone have a crush on Naomi? Or did they have it out for her instead?

———

If Rita was still on duty, Naomi would have an ally. Instead, she had Sara, who might have just stabbed Naomi in the back. But why? What had Naomi done to upset her co-worker?

Nothing came to mind. She hadn't even called the nurse out for being late for her shift. Of course, she didn't log on for Sara either. Naomi couldn't risk her own job for someone who was chronically late. When she really thought about it, Sara had been especially quiet lately. Maybe Naomi had said or done something to turn her co-worker against her. The damage—whatever it was—seemed to have already been done. There was no going back to fix it now. Plus, it was impossible to apologize when she had no idea what she'd done in the first place.

Sara wasn't easy to talk to. She'd been even more difficult to form a bond with. And now Naomi was left scratching her head as to how she'd upset the woman.

Since trying to read someone else's mind was about as productive as trying to get milk from a butterfly, Naomi made a note to watch her back while at work. She thought about the list Harding Quinn had suggested she make. Should Sara's name be on it?

Naomi took out the sheet of paper she'd wadded up and stuffed inside the pouch of her scrubs earlier. She flattened it out using the edge of the counter before locating a pen. The first couple of names on the list came from the dating app: Mario, Raul, Steven, Kevin, and Knox. She'd only gone out with three of them but had had contact with the other two.

Writing the next name down was hard. Theo. The comment about this being personal and someone in her inner circle struck a chord she didn't like. After writing down Theo's name, she issued a sharp sigh and wrote the name Sara. All Naomi's efforts to this point had been aimed at the stalker being a man. The idea this person could be a co-worker sent a cold chill racing down her back.

After writing the names, she folded the piece of paper into a triangle and tucked it inside her pocket instead of the pouch. The risk of losing it while in a patient's room was too great. She tucked too many other things inside the pouch and the paper could come right out without her knowing if she got in a hurry.

Considering the size of scandal that would erupt if she was caught insinuating co-workers might be tormenting her, she had to be very careful. A thin bead of sweat formed on her forehead at the thought of how uncomfortable work would become. She needed this job to pay her bills. It wasn't like she had a trust fund to back her up like some people in this hospital.

Naomi realized she wasn't exactly being fair. The Quinns seemed to be down-to-earth despite their considerable wealth. Harding worked in law enforcement, which wasn't exactly a job he needed. When she thought about it like that, he clearly wasn't doing it for the money. It made her like him even more despite the fact she couldn't afford to.

He did offer to pay her to stay at his place for a couple of days until he got the all-clear. The extra money would come in handy and she could pick his brain in private without all the eyes at the hospital staring at them. She understood on some level that he was the kind of person who drew attention. She'd been naïve to think she could spend time in his room without drawing at least a little suspicion. Handing him over to Sara had been meant to keep Naomi from wanting to wander back in and check on him. She had questions about her circumstances, and he could provide answers.

Maybe she could slip a note inside his room without anyone noticing. Well, now, Naomi really did crack a smile. Folks in this hospital might be clueless as to what went down in the parking lot, but they had the inside of the building covered.

Was she really considering staying at a stranger's house for the next three days? Her only days off?

Harding Quinn wasn't exactly a stranger, a little voice in the back of her mind pointed out. Plus, he worked in law enforcement. She couldn't be with anyone safer than a good person from a decent family who'd made an oath to uphold the law.

Could she do this? Would she be putting her career at risk? There had been instances where nurses hired out for home care. But rumors had apparently already been flying about her spending too much time in Harding's room at the start of her shift.

Dr. Juno rounded the corner, his nose in a chart. He glanced up as she sidestepped him so he wouldn't bump into her.

"Sorry about that," he said, his eyes wide. "I didn't mean to..."

"No worries," she said. "I'm fine. We avoided a collision, so no harm done."

Naomi could use a cup of coffee, so she started toward the break room. Dr. Juno grabbed her arm, stopping her in her tracks. His touch brought a cold chill racing up her arm. Her gut reaction was to jerk her arm free. She stared at the spot where his fingers had been curled around her bicep.

"Excuse me," she said, leaving no room for doubt that he'd crossed a line.

"I'm sorry," he repeated for the second time in less than a minute. He caught her gaze and his forehead creased with concern. "It's just that I overheard Sara talking to one of the other nurses. It was mentioned that you'd spent most of your shift with one patient and since you're a valuable nurse to this floor, I thought it was my duty to warn you."

Dr. Juno seemed like he was genuinely trying to help but she'd gotten the message loud and clear earlier. Naomi prided herself on her professionalism, so it hurt that hers was in question. She wanted nothing more than to point out that she'd been working at the hospital for three years without ever missing a shift or being late, unlike Sara. Saying anything about her co-worker's poor performance would make Naomi look like she was trying to deflect attention. In short, it would make her look like the bad guy.

"Exactly the reason I asked Sara to take over for me in that room," Naomi pointed out, doing her best to keep the defensiveness out of her tone. This seemed like a good time to keep her chin up and a smile on her face.

"Smart idea," Dr. Juno said, bringing his index finger up to his forehead and then tapping.

Naomi didn't like where this was going at all. She needed to ask a trusted source what the rumors about her were, and she knew just who to talk to.

CHAPTER SIX

"Take me home," Harding said to his brother.

"Your supervisor won't like it," Barrett reminded. His brother was thinking logically, whereas Harding was about to lose his mind.

"She'll understand," he countered.

"I'm not so sure about that," Barrett said. "Leaving AMA might land you on desk duty."

"True," Harding agreed. "But staying *with medical advice* will drive me up the wall. If I'm to get any sleep at all, I need my own bed."

"I thought you made a promise to stick around," Barrett said.

"That was when Naomi was my nurse," Harding stated, motioning toward the chalkboard and to the name Sara. "All bets are off now that she took me off her patient list."

"Fair point," Barrett said, pushing up to standing.

"Does this mean what I think?" Harding asked his brother as he tossed his empty coffee cup in the trash.

"Let's find your clothes and get out of here," Barrett said with a dry crack of a smile. "Besides, I'm surprised it took you this long to break out of here."

"It would be nice if I had someone official to take out my IV. Here goes nothing," Harding said before removing the tape on his arm. In one fluid motion, he pulled out his IV. Barrett tossed over gauze and tape.

"You want help?" Barrett asked.

"I got this," Harding reassured as he ripped open the gauze package and then placed the contents on his arm. He bent his elbow to secure the gauze while he managed to pull tape off using his right hand and his teeth. A few seconds later, he was good to go there. Machines were about to start going off. No use trying to unplug them since the critical ones had battery backups.

Hopping to his feet, he grabbed the boxers and jeans his brother held out for him. It only took a few more seconds for him to be in those. He slipped into his boots not bothering with socks.

Barrett was already taking off his flannel shirt. He had on a long sleeve t-shirt underneath that he could get by on. "Based on the location of your injury, I figured they cut you out of yours."

"Yep," Harding confirmed. By the time Sara came storming into the room, Harding was standing at the door. "I'm out of here."

"It's lunch hour around here," Sara said, holding her arms out like she could physically stop Harding from walking out the front door. "Give me a few minutes to run down to the cafeteria and grab your doctor."

"I'm afraid that's not the plan, Sara," Harding said. "Thanks for your help, though."

He stepped past her, got a little woozy as he made it into the hallway. Thankfully, Barrett was right there to grab his arm and prop him up. Harding had always been close with his brother and appreciated his help even more in this moment.

"You can't go without being checked out by the billing department," she countered in a weak argument. Barrett couldn't help but notice the makeup covering a black eye and his heart nearly broke in half. Him leaving the hospital wouldn't hurt her job in any way, so there was no reason for him to feel guilty. But he couldn't come across anyone who was most likely being abused without offering help.

"My department is covering this one, so I'm not the guy to sign off on the bill anyway," Harding started before catching her gaze. "But if you ever want to speak to someone...there are people who would love to help with whatever you're going through."

"Me? I'm good," she said, and there was something hard in her eyes. It was something unreachable. He should know. He'd tried with others without success. Seeing people in abusive relationships stay with an abuser was one of the most difficult aspects of his job. As a U.S. Marshal, he tracked down the most wanted felons to serve arrest warrants. His job took him all over the world. He'd seen abused women and men in every state, every country, and they all had that same hard look until they were ready to break the cycle.

"I can see that you are," he said with as much

compassion as he could find. "And when you're ready to be even better, there are places you can go."

Sara shook her head, refusing to meet his gaze.

Harding knew when he'd lost a fight. He looked around for Naomi and came up empty there too. Glancing over at his brother, he asked, "Ready?"

"Let's roll," Barrett said. His steady hand on Harding got him to the elevator. Once inside, Barrett asked, "Are you doing okay?"

"I just need a shoulder to lean on tonight and then I'll be fine," Harding said. "I'll let the others in the family know once I get home that they can relax."

"I'm guessing you have no plans to tell them how you escaped from the hospital with my help, against medical advice," Barrett said with a chuckle.

"There's no reason for them to worry," Harding said. "I'm good." After the words came out, he recognized them from a few minutes ago. Sara had said the exact same thing and she was clearly not good. This situation might be different, but he recognized the similarity in their stubbornness. He hoped she would get help, and he was determined to do the same. The problem was that the parking lot was full over by the ER where he'd been brought in and Barrett had parked, and he had no idea which vehicle belonged to Naomi.

———

"Can I bug you for a favor?" Naomi asked Hope, who'd been sitting across the cafeteria when Naomi walked in to eat. She'd made a beeline for the floater the second she saw a friendly face.

"Sure, what is it?" Hope asked.

"I need to get a note to a patient without drawing attention and for reasons beyond me there seems to be a spotlight on my activity tonight," Naomi said. "Would you mind delivering a message?"

"Is it true?" Hope asked. The woman never pulled any punches, and Naomi appreciated her for it. She always knew where she stood with Hope, unlike at least one of her other co-workers.

"You'll have to tell me what you're asking before I can confirm or deny any rumors about me," she said.

"You and the Marshal in room 724 striking up a romance," Hope said like she was reading a salacious news headline. Unfortunately, even the lies hurt people.

"Are you seriously asking me if I would do something like that?" Naomi didn't bother to hide the disappointment in her voice.

"Not in a million years would I think it was true," Hope said. "All I wanted was confirmation straight from the horse's mouth." She seemed to realize how that sounded when she smiled, touched Naomi's hand, and added, "You know what I mean to say."

"I do, but it's a frustrating rumor because not everyone knows me. Some people are going to believe it's true and use it to hurt my reputation," Naomi said on a sharp sigh.

"Everyone who truly knows you should realize it's hogwash," Hope said dismissively, but even she had just asked if it was true.

"Why start a rumor like that in the first place?" Naomi asked. Suddenly, her ham sandwich and apple weren't so appetizing.

"To distract people, of course," Hope said without batting an eyelash.

"Why go after me specifically?" she continued, thinking Hope might be onto something here.

"Shock value maybe?" Hope surmised. She was pretty sharp tonight, as always.

"Are you familiar with my recent discussion with Rod asking for parking lot lights?" Naomi asked.

"Now that you mention it, he could be where these flirting rumors are coming from," Hope said. "He can discredit your complaints against him, if you're viewed as someone who is flirting with random men, including patients."

"Are you kidding me right now?" Anger heated Naomi's cheeks, causing her face to flush. She could feel the climb up from her neck to her cheekbones. "In this day and age, a woman can be discredited by calling her a flirt?"

"It's awful, I know," Hope stated, shaking her head before picking up a carrot and chewing on the end. "Not everyone has caught up with the rest of the world."

"Rod definitely fits that description," Naomi said. She zipped her lunch. "I've lost my appetite."

"We'll figure it out," Hope said. "Try not to let him get inside your head in the meantime."

"It's not mine that I'm worried about," she said on a sharp sigh. "It's everyone else's."

Hope's lips compressed in a frown.

"I wish you were wrong," she said. "But at least we know what's real and what isn't."

"I have a good mind to pay Rod a visit," Naomi said. "Tell him exactly what I think about his rumors."

"He's just a guess on my part," Hope said. "Keep your eyes and ears open in case I'm wrong."

"Will do," Naomi said. "And thanks for believing in me."

"Not much gets past me when it comes to people," Hope said with a small smile. It was true. She had a knack for figuring people out.

If Rita hadn't likely been in a deep sleep by now, Naomi would slip into the ER lobby and give her friend a call. In times like these, she almost wished she'd put in to work the day shift. Having the next three days off to reset sounded like heaven about now and the end of her shift couldn't come fast enough as far as she was concerned.

"Let me know if there's anything I can do to help," Hope said.

"Tell me if you hear anything else about me?" Naomi asked.

"You got it, kid," Hope said. She was probably the only person on earth Naomi didn't mind calling her a kid.

"I'm heading back early. I'll take the rest of my break later when I get my appetite back," she said, thinking she wished she could tell Harding about this latest development. He'd promised to have a conversation with Rod.

It would give her time to come up with a strategy of how to deal with him in the future. Hope was right about not going straight at him. Rod couldn't be trusted not to go behind Naomi's back or start more rumors about her.

And then it dawned on her that he must have someone watching her because he should be home asleep this evening. A name came to mind. Theo.

Naomi made a mental note to speak to the orderly. She needed to tread lightly there because she didn't want to spook him and he barely looked her in the eyes at it was. If she didn't approach the conversation right, she might scare him off for good. Plus, she didn't want to cause any discomfort for him. If Rod was using him, she refused to do the same. Handling Theo properly required taking a soft approach. Maybe she could speak to him and dig around for information without being too obvious. He had gone into Harding's room earlier to...what...warn her?

When she really thought about it, he'd come in to not-so-politely ask her to leave the room.

Naomi caught sight of the white-knuckle grip she had going on the strap of her lunch bag in the elevator's mirror. She was still trying to figure out when this shift had gone south. The moment she'd pulled into the parking lot? With her free hand, she fingered the dog tags hanging from the chain around her neck.

The elevator dinged and the doors opened. She rounded the corner to the nurse's station to see Sara and the floor nurse locked in serious conversation. Great. What now? Were the two of them conspiring against her?

There was something else that struck her as odd. The door to room number 724 was wide open. Since she couldn't go inside or ask about it, she moved to the nurse's station instead. As she returned her lunch to the cabinet beside her handbag, another thing hit her between the eyes. Her purse was open. Either Naomi was starting to lose it, or someone had opened her handbag. To what end? What did the person expect to find in there?

She ran inventory on her belongings. There'd been complaints of items missing from handbags in the past month. Nothing out of the ordinary. Most of the time the person complaining found the 'missing' item in the bathroom where they'd set it on the counter and walked off without taking it with them.

Relief washed over her when she saw her wallet inside. Another wave came when she checked for contents. Everything looked in order. Other than that, she had a pair of sunglasses in their case along with breath mints. A couple of pens were lost at the bottom along with spare change. A couple strands of hair and crumbs rounded out the contents. This seemed like a good time to remind herself to clean out her purse.

Since nothing appeared to be missing, she secured her handbag in the cabinet and then locked the door. The only folks who had access to these cabinets were other nurses...a.k.a. Sara. Would she check inside Naomi's personal belongings? There was no money missing and, besides, Naomi was the wrong person to try to steal from on that front. She carried very little cash on her. Mainly enough for the vending machines as a backup in case the credit card feature was broken and she was desperate for a snack. Plus, she didn't have a lot of extra money to waste, so there was that.

Now, she wanted to know why room number 724's

door was open and there seemed to be no activity going on inside. As she took her seat and logged back in the computer, she could hear the voices.

"It was *your* job to keep him here, so tell me again how it is the room is empty and there is no patient inside?" Gwen Givens asked, fists on her hips. Even from this distance of fifteen feet away, the woman's cheeks were blazing red. Not a good sign for Sara, who'd arrived to her shift late. She already had one strike against her. For a split second, Naomi considered marching right over and bringing up the fact to their supervisor. She shot it down just as fast. Sara's antics would catch up to her at some point. Besides, Naomi needed to lie low for a little while and watch her co-worker a little more closely. If Sara was up to something, putting her on the defensive wouldn't help Naomi dig out the truth any faster. In fact, it would slow everything down. And besides, if Sara had it out for Naomi, they would have a standoff soon enough. Naomi could only hope her record and reputation would win out in the end.

Besides, Gwen's words struck like physical blows. Harding was gone? No. She refused to believe he'd walked out after she'd convinced him to stay. A physical ache formed in her chest that was the strongest she'd ever felt, and more familiar than she wanted it to be. All of a sudden, it was like losing Gavin all over again. This was somehow even worse, which made no logical sense considering she'd known Gavin for years and Harding for a few hours.

Still, there was something special about the connection she felt to the Marshal and it was unlike anything she'd experienced in the past. More than ever, she wished she could talk to him and pick his brain as new information was coming in regarding her circumstances.

She knew how to find him...the computer. Was using her work equipment for personal reasons ethical? The billing department would have his home address and his phone number. Could she access the information? She'd never tried to locate a patient once they left the hospital before. He had been her patient first before she'd handed him over to Sara.

Naomi pulled up his chart in the system. The hospital needed a major IT overhaul because its system was ancient. Normally, that frustrated her. Tonight, it might just help her get what she needed, his contact information.

His file was clearly marked with three letters, AMA, which meant he left against medical advice. He had, in fact, done just that so no surprises there. As she skimmed his chart, she saw that he'd been given Percocet. This was a mistake. Naomi glanced at the nurse's initials and found Sara's. There was no way Harding took Percocet. He'd been insistent about not taking anything more than ibuprofen.

Naomi slipped her cell phone out of her pocket and sneaked a picture. She wondered if there was a way to investigate whether or not Sara's patients were the ones complaining about being billed for medications they didn't take. This could explain the uptick in recent inquiries.

She glanced over at Sara as she and Gwen split up. Sara huffed past Naomi and to the cabinet where her lunch was stored. Naomi quickly minimized the screen she'd been working on. If she'd been smart about this, she would have another file opened instead of looking like she was staring at the background screen for no good reason.

Good fortune smiled on her. By the time Sara stormed past again, Naomi had her patient's file on the screen from room 719.

Her sigh of relief was short-lived as she pulled up a couple of recent patient files who'd complained about their bills. Of the two names Naomi remembered, both had been attended by Sara. Was her fellow nurse pocketing pain relievers and billing patients for them? Naomi took a couple more pictures as evidence. Granted, three instances didn't mean Sara was guilty. It did, however, warrant further investigation.

The rest of the shift was long and boring. At least the sun was up by the time Naomi logged herself off the computer and she had the next three days off work. Normally, the thought put a big smile on her face. Not this time. Her thoughts kept shifting to Harding and a big part of her wished she'd taken him up on his offer when it was still available. There was no way to reach him now, she thought as she gathered her things and headed to the elevator bank. On the ride down, the elevator stopped at every floor.

Walking outside, the sun warmed her face despite the chilly air. A cold front was supposed to pass through for the next two days. Then, it would be in the low seventies again in typical Texas fashion.

As Naomi neared her Ford, a knot formed in her gut. A white slip of paper was tucked underneath her windshield wiper blade. Remembering Harding's advice, she would be careful as she picked it up so she wouldn't cover up fingerprints.

She pulled one of the pens from her handbag and used the cap to maneuver the paper out from underneath the blade. Carefully, she unfolded it. *Call me.* Harding's name and cell number were written underneath.

Could she trust this note came from him? Or was this more of a demented person's games?

CHAPTER SEVEN

Harding plumped up the pillow on the couch for the tenth time since sitting down. The TV was on but he wasn't paying attention and, besides, the volume was turned down so low he couldn't hear it anyway. The remote control was right next to him, as was his laptop.

Barrett left for work three and a half hours ago, needing to clock in at the shooting range to keep up his training requirement. His brother would be back in another hour to check on Harding. Making coffee was out of the question without assistance. This helpless feeling was for the birds.

He glanced at the clock. Eleven-fifteen. If she was going to call, she would have done so when she picked up the note Barrett had left on her vehicle last night.

For a split-second, he considered calling HR at the hospital to ask for Naomi's number. But he wouldn't use his career for something personal, so he needed to wrap his mind around the fact she was out of his life. He could admit that it stung more than a little bit that she'd handed him off to another nurse without a word of explanation.

As he reached for the remote, his cell buzzed. He immediately checked the screen. Unknown caller.

"Hello?" he said into the receiver.

"Harding?" came the familiar voice. He exhaled, not realizing he'd been holding his breath.

"Yes, ma'am," he said. "Is this Naomi?"

"It's me. I didn't want to call from the parking lot," she said. His radar shot up.

"Why is that?" he asked.

"Suffice it to say that I had a rough shift and didn't want to draw attention to myself by sitting in the parking lot on the phone," she said.

"Have you reconsidered my offer?" he asked, wanting her to say *yes* more than he wanted to admit.

"We didn't discuss the details," she said. "I'd like to hear more before I commit to anything."

"It's basic stuff that I seem to need help with," he started right in. "Getting from one room to the other. Making coffee, etcetera."

"Showers?" she asked and her voice cracked on the word. She immediately cleared her throat.

"I got those, as long as I can get help into the room," he replied, doing his level best not to react to the thought of the two of them being in an enclosed space for very long.

"What about meals?" She seemed to shift the conversation darn fast.

"My family has my fridge stuffed full of food. An entire professional football team couldn't empty the contents in a week. So, no cooking but there would be heating and plating involved," he said on a chuckle. His family had literally brought home the fatted calf so to speak. Everyone had wanted to contribute something. Since they were restaurant quality cooks, he didn't mind. His freezer was full in the kitchen and the one in his garage was packed as well.

"Good. I don't cook," Naomi said. "But I'm probably pro-level at knowing how long to microwave something."

"Sounds like we're a perfect match," he said before realizing how those words sounded. "In the kitchen."

Adding those last three words didn't make it less awkward. What was up with the high school teenager's nerves?

Harding could admit to being attracted to the beautiful nurse. He could acknowledge it and leave it at that. There'd been plenty of attractive women in his life over the years. They never made him feel this tongue-tied.

"How many days?" she asked.

"I'd like all three if that's on the table," he said. "It's not twenty-four-hour care in the sense of needing to do something every minute. I'd appreciate the company but I'll sleep a solid seven hours at night, so no worries there. And you don't have to entertain me while you're here. I'd like to discuss your case. See if we can come up with a solution there or at the very least get an investigation started with the right agency or point you in the right direction should anything else show up on your vehicle. That's all I can think of for now but there's probably more along those same lines."

She was quiet for a long moment and he hoped that meant she was seriously contemplating his offer.

"The pay is twenty-four hundred dollars a day, which breaks down to a hundred dollars an hour," he added.

"Wow," she said low and under her breath. "That's a down payment on a new car."

"Is it a deal?" he asked, hoping to capitalize on the moment.

"You could get someone for a whole lot less money," she stated.

"Maybe. But I want the best and you should be paid for your work," he insisted, and meant it. Had he gone too far? Money was the least important thing in his life. If it could help someone else, he'd gladly give it away. In this case, Naomi would earn every penny by committing to work on her days off.

"Text your address," she said. "I need to stop by my home first so I can pack a bag."

"Done," he said, realizing his grin was ear-to-ear at this point. He reined it in before he came across as a heart-sick teenager. "I'll see you when you get here."

"Sounds good," she said. "And thank you. I can really use someone to talk to after what happened at work last night."

Those words brought him back to reality.

"We can go over the details once you arrive," he said.

"Okay," she said, and for the first time during the conversation he thought the nervous tension he'd picked up in her voice might not have anything to do with the thought of spending the next three days with him.

A new, safer vehicle was a whole lot closer with the job she'd taken from Harding Quinn. She would have been a fool to refuse it. The fact she would be getting free advice from him didn't quite seem fair. She would shave some off the price of her services in exchange for his guidance.

Naomi lived fifteen minutes from the hospital and she'd pulled over at the gas station on her block to call Harding, so it only took another five before she walked in her door. She'd jumped through the shower and packed a bag in half an hour. In a rare move, she applied concealer to hide the bags under her eyes and a tinted lip gloss. Blow drying her hair took a few minutes more as did a change of clothes. She threw on yoga pants and a sports bra, then a light sweater. Cold weather and Texas went together about as well as salsa and vanilla yogurt. A couple of minutes later, she was out the door.

The drive into Austin was a beating, as expected. Midday traffic was as bad as she remembered and also the reason she worked and lived outside the city. She couldn't imagine navigating through this every day. Cars zipped in and around her like they were on a hot track. Trucks were pushy. The drivers seemed to think they could intimidate her to change lanes, which she would gladly do to get out of their way if cars would let her in. The term bumper-to-bumper was coined in conditions like these. A couple of horns blared but for the most part, drivers seemed to give in.

She did her best to drive with the flow, as the GPS on her phone directed her. Traffic thinned as she moved past the downtown area and to Travis City, which was a huge relief. It was short-lived when she realized a white two-door sedan had been tracking her movements, following her. The knot that had formed in her gut earlier tightened as though people stood on each end tugging the rope.

Naomi pulled in front of an end unit two-story townhouse, slowed down, and checked her rearview. GPS indicated she had arrived at her destination. The white vehicle had a dent on the right side in the front. The headlight had been crushed in the accident. There were no plates. The law required plates on the front and back of the vehicle but that didn't necessarily translate. A lot of cars and trucks only had plates in back. The only reason she knew about the law was that she'd been pulled over for it once. Thankfully, the cop wasn't a stickler but he he'd pointed out that he was giving her a pass if she promised to affix the plate when she got home. She did and she had.

The white vehicle didn't slow down as it passed by her. She realized just how paranoid she'd become when she saw the driver. Unless Naomi was being followed by a seventy-year-old grandmother, she was in the clear.

After parking in the visitor lot across from the front door of Harding's townhouse, Naomi grabbed her overnight bag before heading to the door. Rather than knock, she texted to let him know she'd arrived. It occurred to her that she hadn't told him what kind of vehicle she drove. There was no way he could have known the Ford belonged to her.

A text message came almost immediately, telling her to come on inside. She wondered about his decision to leave his door unlocked while he was in a weakened state.

"Hi," she said after walking inside. She closed and locked the door behind her.

"Thank you for coming," he said. "You just missed my brother. Barrett left about five minutes ago. He said to tell you hello."

"That's nice of him," she said, wondering what it was really like to come from such a big family. "Please let him know that I said to tell him hello back." She remembered what Harding had said about the packed refrigerator, full of food. Based on what she'd seen and heard so far, the pluses outweighed the downsides by a mile.

"I'd get up and give you a tour if I could," he said. "As it is, your room is upstairs. First door on the right." She must have given him quite the look because he added, "I'm taking the guest room downstairs, figuring it'll be easier if I stick to one floor."

"Right," she said with a sigh of relief. Sleeping in a room next to Harding shouldn't have caused a dozen butterflies to release in her stomach the way it did. He was a patient and she was a professional. She'd never gone out with anyone from work before and had no plans to start now.

"Why don't you put your stuff in your room and then you can fill me in on what happened," he said.

"Okay," she said, thinking she was really winning with her one-word answers. Putting patients at ease around her was usually one of her gifts. Why was she thrown off-kilter with Harding? He was a man like any other. A voice in the back of her mind picked that moment to point out Harding Quinn was unlike any man Naomi had ever seen or heard of. She cracked a smile. It was true.

The only way to get through the next three days was to distance herself from her emotions, something she'd become a master at, and focus on the patient's needs.

Gripping the handle of her bag, she crossed the large living area and into the adjacent open-concept dining room. Stairs were to the right, so she made the trek up. Harding's home didn't look anything like she expected a U.S. Marshal's to. It was funny now that she really thought about it, but part of her had expected there to be a black leather couch, black and white art on the walls, and practically nothing else. What she found instead was a sectional sofa in warm tones, with coordinating throw pillows and a blanket draped over the back. The white marble coffee table had a plant on it that sat on top of a stack of hardback books. There was a blown-glass vase that had the most interesting blues and greens mingled throughout. The large flatscreen TV was affixed to the adjacent wall, and a TV had been expected, but instead of wires sticking out everywhere, there was a wide sideboard table pushed up against the wall with even more books.

In this moment, she felt more than a little embarrassed to have lumped Harding into a category with a narrow description. It was obvious the man liked to read based on the sheer number of books throughout his home. Why wouldn't a U.S. Marshal read?

Shaking off the mortification that came with pigeonholing someone, she stepped into a generous-sized bedroom. The four-poster bedframe on what looked like a full-size bed had a canopy. There were feminine touches everywhere, from the desk that faced the window with a velvet teal-colored chair pushed up to it to the fluffy white throw pillows on the bed.

The reason dawned on her. A girlfriend or ex-wife must have helped decorate the place. Or, it could have been someone who wanted to be a girlfriend. No matter. Naomi wasn't here to start a relationship with anyone. Besides, even if she was attracted to Harding, there was no way she intended to date anyone who worked in another dangerous job. Losing Gavin had cemented the thought and her mind was made up.

She did, however, want to pick Harding's brain about everything going on at work. Setting her bag on a side chair near the bed, she closed the door after exiting the room. The door to the master was wide open and the overwhelming temptation to peek inside surprised her. Since she'd never been a snoop, she pushed the instinct aside and headed back downstairs.

Harding was in the exact same spot as she left him. Had he moved much at all since arriving home last night?

"First things first," she began, figuring she needed to make it clear that she intended to earn her keep. "How did you sleep?"

"Better than I would have if I'd stayed in the hospital," he stated, motioning for her to sit down on the opposite end of the couch. "Before we get into the details, would you mind putting on a pot of coffee? Only if you're not too tired after being on your feet all night. Because if you are, you're welcome to take a nap. I can hold off on caffeine a little while longer. Otherwise, I hope you'll make yourself at home and join me in a cup."

"Coffee sounds like heaven," she said, redirecting toward the kitchen. The large marble island was beyond gorgeous. The art on the walls couldn't necessarily be described as modern, but the colors were warm with pops of blue and green that highlighted the blown glass vase. It was tempting to ask if he'd dated a decorator at some point. In the hospital, he'd told Dr. Juno that he was single. Living alone wasn't the same as being single. He could be dating someone but the relationship wasn't serious enough to warrant a home care request. Maybe it was in the early stages. Why did the thought practically gut her?

The coffee pot was the old-fashioned variety. She'd expected one of those pod machines but was pleasantly surprised by the standard carafe type on the counter. Other than the coffee maker, there wasn't a whole lot on the countertops. A jar marked coffee sat next to the machine. Easy-peasy. She had a pot brewed in a matter of minutes after realizing the filter was one of those reusable kinds.

She had no idea what kind of grinds he used because the room filled with an aroma that was otherworldly. After checking the cabinets and finding mugs in the one above the machine, she filled them with the fresh brew. It was times like these that she reminded herself to slow down and breathe, allow herself to be amazed at how the little things could fill her soul with happiness.

Mug in each fist, she returned to the living room.

"I probably should have asked how you take your

coffee," she said. "Thought I remembered something from last night about—"

"Black," he stated.

"I had a feeling when I smelled the grounds," she said with a small smile.

"Same for you, or were you too timid to open the fridge?" he asked.

"Why ruin the taste with sugar?" she asked. "Mind if I sit?"

"Please," he said. "Make yourself comfortable. I wasn't kidding. For the next three days, *mi casa es su casa.*"

As great as it sounded—his house was her house—she reminded herself this was a temporary job. It would be a mistake to get too comfortable here. And her heart warned it could be dangerous.

CHAPTER EIGHT

"I'm surprised you didn't sleep better after taking a Percocet last night," Naomi said before taking a sip of coffee, her gaze stayed trained on Harding the whole time.

"What are you talking about?" he asked. He would have known if he took something stronger than ibuprofen.

"Your chart said you caved and finally took serious pain medication," she said with a raised eyebrow. Even dressed casually in yoga pants and a sweater, she looked beautiful. Her creamy skin wasn't something he needed to notice. Not now. Not ever. He especially didn't need his gaze to drop to those full pink lips of hers.

"Then Sara must have marked it wrong because I refused her in pretty much the same manner as I did you," he said, thinking it was more likely she'd marked the chart for her own benefit instead.

"Sorry about that, by the way," Naomi said with more than a hint of guilt in her tone. "I didn't mean to pawn you off on Sara. The rumor Theo mentioned when he came in the room concerned me. I can't afford to lose my job, not even with a good paying side gig like this one. Wealthy cattle ranchers turned Marshals who've been injured don't come around every day or offer health insurance."

Harding chose to ignore the comment despite how much it stung. Being lumped in the privileged rancher category sat hard in his gut. And yet, he couldn't or wouldn't deny that he'd been fortunate to be on the receiving end of a whole lot of cash. To him, money didn't equate to passion. His job was his life and he was proud of his accomplishments, none of which had been handed to him.

"Did you figure out who started the rumor?" he asked, realizing Sara's name should probably go on their list now.

She shook her head.

"I'm starting to think my co-worker is sabotaging me, though, to draw attention away from her," she said. "There have been complaints from patients after release that they are being billed for pain medication they never took. I searched her case files, which could get me in trouble. I probably shouldn't even admit it to you."

That got his attention.

"That's not just being bad at her job. It's illegal if she's pocketing those pills," he said, ignoring her last remark. They weren't on the record and she hadn't done anything illegal as far as he was concerned.

"It got me wondering whether or not she is taking

them personally, or stealing for someone else," she stated.

"The eye," he said. "I noticed her black eye and it concerned me enough that I asked her if she wanted to speak to someone to get help. Based on her behavior and the bruises on her arms, it seems to me that abuse is likely going on at home."

"I saw that too. Her husband could be pressuring her to take the pills from work," Naomi reasoned. "They argue a lot. Rita and I have overheard Sara fighting on the phone during her break more times than we can count."

Harding nodded.

"I wouldn't be surprised one bit if her husband is pressuring her for the pills if she's not taking them herself," he said, thinking Naomi was perceptive for a civilian. Then again, she'd probably seen a whole lot more than the average person given her profession in the medical field.

"Sara might be feeding me into the gossip mill to draw attention away from her," Naomi said. "She's been late for work a lot recently too. She knows I won't cover. I mean, I won't give her up or tell on her, but I won't log her onto the computer and make it look like she's there when she isn't."

"Has she asked you to do that?" he asked, figuring he already knew the answer. In his line of work, it was best not to assume anything. Even if the answer was obvious to him and everyone around, he still asked the question. Because there was always that one time in a hundred the answer took him in a whole new direction. Bottom

line? A good investigator asked questions he thought he
already knew the answer to.

"Not directly, no. She has hinted that it would be
really helpful if 'someone' logged her in, but she never
made eye contact, so I was able to pretend that I didn't
hear her and move on," she said. "The subject never
came up again."

"When did this go down?" he asked.

"A couple of months ago," she said. "Sara used to be
a lot better about being on time. She seemed to care a
lot more about doing a good job at work too."

"When did the so-called gifts arrive on your vehicle?" he asked.

"Within the last couple of weeks," she stated.

He nodded, thinking the timing was suspect. The
heat seemed to be turning up on Sara's situation and
then suddenly rumors start about Naomi, while 'gifts'
show up on her vehicle.

"Did you start the list we talked about?" he asked.

"Yes," she said, and then surprised him by pulling a
folded up sheet of paper out of her pocket. She
smoothed out the corners and placed it on the coffee
table.

"Add Sara's name," he suggested.

"I already did," she admitted, surprising him with
the admission. Naomi would make a solid investigator.

"Good move," he said. "Any other names on there
that I should know about?"

She pushed the list toward him so he could reach
for it.

"This might sound incredibly naïve, but it's strange

to believe any of my co-workers could have it out for me like this," she said on a sigh.

"The person could be trying to scare you into being quiet. We'll focus on the dates from the app you mentioned first. See what we come up with there. Sara's activities could be unrelated but she can't go unchecked. Not if she is stealing opioids from work," he said before digging into a personal question that had been on his mind since Naomi had first walked into his room at the hospital. "Can I ask who the dog tags you're wearing belong to?"

"These?" she asked, sounding more than a little caught off guard.

"If it's none of my business or too personal, don't be afraid to say so," he quickly added.

She sat there for a long moment fingering the tags.

"Well, these are personal. Suffice it to say they're unrelated to what's going on today," she said and he could feel a wall come up between them as she crossed her legs and folded her arms over her chest. The meaning behind her wearing those tags was even more intense than he realized. It was probably for the best he'd decided not to pursue any attraction toward her. The dog tags said it all and he feared he'd be competing for her attention with a ghost. That would be a losing proposition if ever there was one.

"That's all I needed to hear," he said, trying to salvage the momentum they'd had going before his question.

Naomi stood up.

"I need a refill," she said, not making eye contact. "How's your cup?"

"Good for now," he said, realizing he'd just seriously overstepped his bounds. Exactly the reason he decided to change the subject for the time being. "Have you eaten dinner yet?"

"As a matter of fact, no," she admitted from his kitchen. Seeing her there looked a little too right, but he reminded himself that Dog Tags would always be in the way. If she couldn't talk about the owner there was no way she was ready to move on from him.

———

Naomi rolled her shoulders to ease some of the tension that had formed at Harding's question about Gavin's dog tags. No one knew the details about him, not even Rita and she was Naomi's best friend. Or at least as close as Naomi ever let anyone get to her. It had been her for so long, taking care of herself. Letting others in proved harder than she ever imagined it would be.

The knot in her stomach jumped up to her shoulders, drawing them together until it felt like her muscle might snap. *Breathe.*

"I wrote down the handful of names from the dating app. They're all on there," she said from the kitchen, needing to be away from Harding's strong male presence a few seconds longer. As it was, she wanted to lean into him, into his strength. The past year had been more difficult than she'd ever imagined. She'd been surviving each day the best she could. Dating was turning into a disaster. No matter how many times Rita told Naomi she needed to 'get out there' and 'get back in the game,' it wasn't happening.

"It would be nice if we had their screen names," he said.

"The name of the dating app is on there too, if you want to check it out," she stated. After a sip of coffee, she was ready to rejoin Harding in the living room. Through the slightly opened slats in the blinds covering the front picture window, she saw a vehicle idling next to her Ford. Head down, a male figure returned to the driver's side. From this vantage point, she couldn't make out what he looked like or was doing outside of his vehicle a few seconds ago. A hoodie covered most of his head.

Naomi raced to the front door.

"What's happening?" Harding asked. From the corner of her eye, she saw him reach in between the cushion and the base of the sofa. Was he retrieving a weapon? She supposed that the man did work in law enforcement.

"Someone was stopped in front of my SUV," she said as she made it to the front door.

Harding was already pushing to his feet. He took a couple of steps before dizziness seemed to catch up with him. Throwing out a hand, he caught himself against the wall as she unlocked and then opened the door.

"What do you see?" he asked.

"Dark truck. Could be black or navy blue," she reported as he managed to join her.

He shook his head like a dog straight from a bath. The move seemed to work as color returned to his cheeks.

"He's gone," she said as the truck disappeared

around the corner. The engine revved as the truck sped off.

"Are you sure the driver is male?" he asked.

"He wasn't big like you, in that sense, and he was wearing a hoodie so I couldn't get any details of his face or hair color," she said. "But the driver had the build of a man. Long legs, broader chest. I'd say he was shy of six feet tall, but not by much."

At six feet four inches, Harding would tower over the driver who was long gone by now. It would do no good to try to run after him.

"Let me walk you out to your SUV," Harding said, tucking a weapon in the waistband of his jeans. He pulled out his flannel shirt to cover the butt.

"I'm sure the safety is engaged on that thing," she said.

"I can do one better. I have on a special holster that clips into the waistband of my jeans," he said. "I don't go anywhere without carrying, since I can be called to serve a warrant at various hours of the day or night."

"Why don't you put a hand on my shoulder to steady yourself?" Naomi took a step outside, and was pleased Harding followed her close behind. His hand dwarfed her shoulder, but she didn't mind. It was the buzz of electricity humming through her body at the point of contact that threw her off. The initial jolt was one thing. The intensity was enough to power half the city but what followed was a warmth that cascaded over her like a gentle waterfall. It left behind a trail of tingles and sensations she'd never experienced from one touch before.

And she should have. She'd been engaged to be

married to Gavin. She'd planned to spend the rest of her life with him despite never experiencing anything like this when they touched. Then again, she'd had no idea what she was missing until now.

With Gavin, everything had been familiar. There'd been such a comfort in being with someone who knew her longer than six months or a year, unlike her other relationships. The two of them went all the way back to high school when they'd been lovestruck kids. She'd been in the bleachers rooting for him when he'd tossed up the winning layup, a second before the buzzer to give their school its first playoff victory in fifteen years. Gavin had been her first kiss, her first love, and her, well, first.

Parting ways after high school had seemed like the smart move. There'd been a conversation she vaguely remembered about each of them needing to go find themselves. Looking back, all she thought about was the time they'd wasted apart. She could have had so many more years with him if they'd stayed together and gotten married like they'd considered. By now, they might have had a couple of kids.

The loss of their planned life together was as awful as the day she'd lost him.

Harding squeezed her shoulder and the move brought her back to the present and out of her heavy thoughts. Traffic hummed on the roads around the townhouse complex. She listened for the vroom of the engine from a few moments ago. Dread settled around her shoulders like a winter cloak.

The timing of the truck didn't exactly rule out her co-worker, but Sara drove an older minivan. Naomi searched her memory for the vehicles of her dates. Two of them had parked farther away from the busy coffee shop where they'd met for her attempt at screening candidates before committing to a dinner date.

"Let's take a look together," Harding encouraged, his words soothed her more than she wanted to allow.

As they crossed the lane on the interior road of the complex, she almost immediately saw something on her windshield. Had the truck followed her? It was the only thing that made sense, especially with the way the driver had bolted out of there as though he'd been on a mission. The thought occurred to her that he could be a messenger of some sort and possibly not the actual person behind the 'gifts.'

Would her stalker be cavalier enough to put something on her vehicle while she was at the home of a U.S. Marshal?

"I'm surprised he found me here," she said to Harding. "Or, should I say that I'm even more shocked he would put something on my vehicle while I'm with you."

"It does shift the focus of the investigation away from someone at the hospital," he stated.

She really was scratching her head now. A sense of relief should probably wash over her at the possibility someone from work wasn't responsible for the 'gifts.' The idea someone from work could dislike her enough to want to torture her sat hard on her chest. At least this way she could feel safe around her co-workers if it turned out none of them were involved.

"It's a notecard," she said, confused at the message. There were two words written on it: *Go home.*

"I have a pair of tweezers in the drawer on the right of the master bedroom. Would you mind grabbing them for me?" Harding asked.

"No problem," she said, realizing he didn't want to mess up the possibility of fingerprints being on the card. The first real sign of hope struck that she might be making progress on uncovering her stalker's identity. Could she risk hope?

CHAPTER NINE

Harding used the tweezers to pluck the notecard out from underneath the windshield wiper of Naomi's SUV. The message was pretty clear. Her stalker didn't want her going to anyone else's home. Another man's? This led him back to the list of men she'd interacted with, worked with, or dated.

"What do we do next?" Naomi asked.

"Get me back inside and make a call to Austin PD," he said. "This is their jurisdiction and I don't want to step on any toes."

"I don't technically live in Austin, though," she pointed out.

"The crime occurred here," he said, knowing full well claiming that a message left on her vehicle telling her to go home was a stretch to call a threat. "Crime is a strong word, though. I view this as a threat given everything else I know about what has been happening, but Austin PD might not view it the same way. Plus, I'd have to hand over the evidence, which could end up lost, since they would likely view this as a nuisance complaint more than anything else."

He was thinking out loud as they made their way back to his townhouse.

"This is exactly the reason I didn't call the law before when the so-called gifts showed up. Rod in security had twisted the whole situation to make me think I was the one being paranoid," Naomi said as she closed and locked the door behind them.

Harding needed to think for a minute. The walk to the SUV and back had reminded him that he'd been in surgery less than two days ago. Thankfully, the surgery had been minor and he'd narrowly escaped being in real trouble with the bullet fragment. The arrest warrant hadn't been served and a felon was on the loose. Not exactly warm and fuzzy thoughts, but Harding or one of the other Marshals would find Ned Barker. The man would stand in front of a jury and have his fate read in a court of law.

"Would you mind grabbing a paper bag from the drawer in the kitchen?" Harding asked.

Naomi's eyebrow shot up as she nodded.

"It's the best way to hold onto evidence without contaminating it," he explained.

After opening a couple of drawers, she returned with a white paper bag. He took the offering and their fingers grazed, sending a shock of electricity rocketing through him. The same thing had happened when he touched her shoulder. This unwelcomed distraction needed to hop in the backseat because he didn't have the time or focus for it.

Harding placed the evidence in the bag, set the

tweezers down on the coffee table, and then removed his weapon, before tucking it safely in the spot carved out underneath the couch cushion. He leaned back. When he really thought about it, the note could be interpreted any number of ways.

"What are you thinking?" Naomi asked.

"I'm trying to decide if calling in the police is such a good idea after all," he said before outlining his thoughts.

"Those are the same reasons that I haven't called them in," she said. "There hasn't been a direct threat, even though this feels a whole lot like one. Rod got inside my head a little more than I would like. I don't believe that I'm overreacting but the rest of the world might. Aside from you." She paused. "Thank you, by the way."

He shot a confused look at her.

"For listening to me and taking this seriously," she said.

"I wouldn't be good at my job if I didn't," he stated.

Her lips thinned and he couldn't help the feeling he'd just said something wrong.

"Do you want to park your SUV in my garage around back while you're here?" he asked. It would be so easy to use his work resources but also unethical. Those were off limits unless an official investigation was opened and there was a reason for him to get involved. He couldn't ask Barrett, either. He had a brother who was a cop in Houston, a whole lot of good that did. On his side of the family five out of five brothers worked in law enforcement and no one could help.

"That's a good idea. I'd prefer if no one knows my

business," she stated. "On the other hand, it also frustrates me to let this jerk feel like he won."

"Believe me, I understand," he said. "I'd feel the same way."

She issued a sharp sigh.

"I'll grab my keys," she said. "Do you think it's a good idea to go now or should I wait until dark?"

"He just acted, so he probably won't circle back around for at least a little while until he thinks it's safe to do so," he said. "He knows we'll be watching out now. Since he tried to slip the note on your vehicle undetected, he doesn't want to get caught or be seen doing it. The hoodie also signifies that he is trying to hide his identity."

"I'll go move my SUV right now," she said.

He pushed up to standing and then sat right back down.

"Don't move," she said as her forehead wrinkled in concern.

"I have to get up and walk at some point," he countered with a forced smile. "Now seemed like a good time."

"This isn't a good time to bust your stitches," she warned.

"Right. I'll make a note not to do that," he quipped. His attempt at humor fell flat. "How about this...I promise to be careful."

"There's no convincing you to sit there while I handle everything, is there?" she asked with a hand on her hip.

"It sounds bad when you put it like that," he said, making another attempt to lighten the mood. Tension radiated from her in waves and he hoped to be the one to help her calm down again.

Finally, a small smile broke through.

"You really are as stubborn as I thought you would be," she said.

"I had to give you a reason to earn your pay, didn't I?" he quipped, hoping to capitalize on the moment and bring her stress down a couple more notches.

"Little did I know you were underpaying me," she stated with a sober face. And then she broke into a small smile.

"So you do have a sense of humor in there," he said, relaxing a little more as he pushed up to standing. This time, he held his balance for longer than two seconds.

"One I promise to keep, if *you* promise not to hurt yourself," she said.

"Sounds like a fair deal," he stated. Standing came a little easier this time. He also realized he hadn't taken any pain reliever in longer than four hours. This was progress. He'd take it. He reached for his gun and then tucked it inside the waistband of his jeans just in case.

"I'll meet you around back then," she said.

"After I see that you make it safely to your vehicle."

She smiled. "Good plan," she said after retrieving her keys and heading out the front door.

He stood there using his hands to anchor himself in the doorframe. Skimming the area, he searched for any sign of the truck. Came up empty. Whoever was stalking her kept to the shadows. The person preferred slinking around in the fringes, hiding his face. It also indicated this person didn't want to get caught. Was the note a sign he was escalating, though? It took a lot of bravado to follow her here from the hospital. Had the person been in the parking lot of her work after her shift?

This person had to have memorized her schedule. He could have waited on a nearby street for her to leave work. Harding needed to put some serious thought into the case. He would also have to break through the pain fog. He bit back a yawn. Lack of sleep wasn't helping matters.

He glanced at the clock on the wall after Naomi was safely in the driver's seat. How had two hours already passed?

Despite drinking coffee, she had to be wiped out after a twelve hours shift that kept her on her feet most of the time. Harding made his way to the kitchen. At least he was moving a little faster this time and without someone to lean on. Granted, he'd had to grab the wall for support along the way but he'd made it. He moved through the small laundry area and to the garage before hitting the button to let her in.

The Ford was nowhere to be found. He listened for the sound of an engine as panic set in. Should he have gotten inside the vehicle with her? Had someone blocked her from entering the small alleyway?

Frustration and fear nailed his gut as he hoofed it out of the garage and into the alley. Naomi was nowhere in sight and his heart pounded against the inside of his ribcage.

———

Naomi bit back a swear word. She'd turned left instead

of right into Harding's alley when she saw a black truck idling at the light across the street. She'd whipped the steering wheel in the opposite direction in the hopes of getting a license plate. However, the teenager behind the wheel couldn't possibly have been driving the same truck. She'd looked all of seventeen years old.

Making a U-turn, her cell buzzed. She glanced down and saw Harding's name. He must be worried sick. She tapped the green button on the screen, glanced down for a few seconds, and then slammed her brakes to stop herself from hitting the car in front of her.

Naomi's nerves were fried. Despite downing two cups of coffee, she bit back a yawn as she answered the call.

"Where are you?" Harding asked in a controlled-calm voice. This was probably not a good sign.

"I'm at the light. I thought I saw him," she said by way of explanation.

"So you decided to go off half-cocked without me to chase him? Then what? Follow him? To go where? Possibly some place he *wanted* you to go. Somewhere more secluded," he stated. This time, she could hear the fear in his tone that he seemed to be trying to cover and she felt awful for putting him through those few minutes of not knowing where she was or what had happened to him. "That was a dangerous move, Naomi."

"Hearing it like that makes me realize that I could have been playing right into his hand," she said. He was still so calm in the face of danger whereas her pulse was pounding. And when she thought about how close she might have just come to giving her stalker the advantage he was looking for, she felt even worse. "Next time, I'll think before I act."

"Promise me there won't be a next time," he said low and under his breath. For the first time she realized just how unsettled he'd been by the experience.

"Okay," she said, knowing full well it was a promise she might not be able to keep. The only thing she could control was her actions. The truck was a wild card. "I'm turning into the alley now."

"Would you mind staying on the line until I see you," he requested.

"I'm here," she said, pulling into the opening. The sight of him standing there, leaning against the door-jamb for support caused an ache in her chest like nothing she'd ever known. It was a longing so deep she would never find the floor, so intense that it robbed her breath.

She'd only been at Harding's home for a few hours and yet she felt right at home. Being here with him shouldn't feel like the most natural thing or like the mixed up world had somehow righted itself. And yet, that's exactly what happened. No matter how much her logical mind protested falling for Harding, her trai-torous heart had other ideas. Because she *was* falling for him. Hard. How on earth would she survive three days with her heart still intact when she walked out the front door?

Harding immediately hit the button to close the garage door once she put the gearshift in park and cut the engine. Taking in a deep breath to fortify her, she exited the SUV. A force that seemed outside of her caused her to walk straight to him and into an embrace.

He winced as her arms wrapped around his midsection and yet stopped her from pulling away.

"I promise to take a step back and think before I act again, but I need your word on something too," she said to him.

"For what?" he asked as he tightened his grip around her. She tried not to think about how right it felt to be in his arms where she could hear the staccato rhythm of his heart.

"Give me your word that you'll listen to my advice, and not push yourself too hard over the next couple of days," she said.

"All I can say is that I'll try," he said honestly. "I'm not made to sit around and wait for much of anything, including healing from an injury. I may not have taken a bullet before but I grew up rough and tumble, and I have a good sense of what it takes for my body to heal. Plus, I have every intention of catching the..." he seemed to choose his next words carefully, "person stalking you."

Interesting that he didn't say the man who was stalking her. Did he still believe it was possible Sara was behind this?

"Do we have a deal?" she pressed. "I don't run off half-cocked and you let me take care of you, so you can heal properly."

"Yes," he said. "I'll do my best to listen and obey."

"Good," she said. "We can start by getting you to bed. When was the last time you took ibuprofen?"

"I was just asking myself the same question. It had to be longer than four hours ago. I'm thinking six or seven," he stated.

"And you're on your feet?" she didn't hide her incredulity. "You're more like a machine than a man if you're still standing after what little pain medication you've taken has already worn off."

Harding laughed and it was a low rumble in his chest.

"That's probably true," he said.

"One a scale of one to ten, how's the pain?" she asked.

"Right now? I'd say a healthy six," he stated.

"Then you really aren't human," she teased, easing the tension that had built up in the garage. "Let's get you inside, medicated, and to bed."

Now, a slow grin spread across perfectly straight, perfectly white teeth.

"I thought you'd never ask," he said.

Naomi laughed. She couldn't help herself. "Okay, funny guy. Inside."

"Your wish is my command," he said. His comment sent a wave of need racing through her. And just like a tsunami, Harding would devastate her when this was all said and done. Besides, an attraction to him felt like the worst betrayal to Gavin because she'd never felt this way toward her late fiancé.

CHAPTER TEN

Harding felt the instant the air changed between him and Naomi. Every time the two of them got close, she put up a wall.

"Let's get you inside," she said. Her tone had shifted too. She sounded detached in a way that he couldn't explain and wouldn't know where to start if he tried. He didn't like it because his worst fear was that the change in her demeanor had to do with the dog tags hanging around her neck; a subject she'd been clear was off limits.

"I'm fine," he said, leaning on the wall instead of her.

"Okay," she responded. "Tell me where your ibuprofen is and I'll grab a few for you."

"There's a bottle in the pantry over there," he nodded toward the door that was cracked open. He got it. Her relationship status was complicated.

"Thanks," she said, easing away from him as he made his way over to the kitchen table to sit down.

The main problem he had was that he actually liked

holding Naomi. For a split second, the world had righted itself and he felt like he was exactly where he should be. His cell buzzed in his pocket. He fished it out and checked the screen.

"Everything okay?" Naomi asked as she returned from the pantry, medicine bottle in hand. She dished out four tablets onto the table and then located a glass before filling it with water. She set it on the table, locking gazes with him when he didn't answer.

"It's one of my brothers threatening to come over," he said with a half smile.

"That's nice of him," she said, taking a seat opposite him.

"The Quinns stick together," he admitted, wondering who had her back. She caught his gaze and the coil in his chest tightened. He could stare into those violet eyes of her all day. Harding coughed to ease the sudden dryness in his throat. Breaking eye contact would be the best play right now but nothing in him wanted to do it. Reminding himself that her heart seemed to belong to Dog Tags finally did the trick.

"That must be nice," she said, not with anger or jealousy, but with a softness and gentleness that told him she'd never truly experienced it.

Harding picked up the pills, tossed them in his mouth and then dry-swallowed all four. After, he picked up the water and drained the contents. Staying hydrated would help him get on his feet faster.

"I'll be fine for a while by myself," he said. "Why don't you go upstairs and rest?"

"What are you going to do while I sleep?" she asked.

"Work on my laptop. Watch a game that I have

recorded. Take a nap on the couch," he said but she'd started shaking her head after the first couple of words.

"Healing requires rest," she said. "I see that you're a tough guy. It's beyond anything I've witnessed that you're already up and around at all, not to mention without pain medication. But the only way to truly heal is to close your eyes for longer than a few minutes."

"I will," he said.

It must have occurred to her this was prime awake time for him.

"Then, I'll stay up with you," she said, glancing over at the clock. "It'll be dinner time in the next hour or so. Then, a shower for you. I'll have another cup of coffee to hold me over."

At that moment, she yawned.

"Would it make you happy if I showered and we ate early?" he asked.

"Food first. And only if you'll promise to work on your laptop in bed," she said with a determined look in her eye.

"You drive a hard bargain," he said.

"I'm being handsomely paid to take care of you. Remember?" she asked with a smile.

He couldn't argue there, so he waited for her to heat up a couple plates of lasagna. They polished them off quickly and he realized he was hungrier than he thought.

"Since I took off against medical advice, no one gave me a self-care sheet on showering with stitches," he said.

"That'll be easy," she said, pushing to her feet. "Which drawer has Saran Wrap?"

"The one closest to the fridge." He motioned toward it.

She crossed the room, retrieved the Saran Wrap, and then returned with a self-satisfied smile on her face. "Lift up your arms but be careful as you do. Get them up as high as you can without hurting yourself."

Harding raised his elbows up until he could hold his palms out level with the tile floor. He forced a smile.

Naomi unbuttoned his flannel shirt one at a time before helping him shrug out of it.

"You can use a washcloth on this area once you're out of the shower," she said as her voice cracked. She cleared her throat before continuing. "I'll just wrap you with Saran Wrap to keep this section dry. We can change your bandages once you're finished showering."

Her fingers on his body felt better than they should. He probably shouldn't focus on the fact Naomi touching him felt like the most natural thing, and yet it was all he could think about.

"Do you need help getting undressed?" she asked. Her violet eyes glittered with something that looked a whole lot like need. Since the signals she sent were as confusing as all get out, he took in a slow breath before shaking his head.

"I've got this," was all he said.

"Okay," she said as she tucked in the edge of the wrap. "Yell if you need me. I'll be right outside the door."

Harding started to protest but she stopped him.

"It's my job, Harding," she said. "Let me do what you hired me to in order to earn my paycheck. I won't feel right taking money from you otherwise."

When she put it like that, it only sounded fair.

"I might come from a big family who always had each other's backs, but I think that gave us all an independent streak a mile long," he said by way of explanation. "We all became even more determined to make it through life not needing to lean on anyone else. We are a stubborn bunch."

"Being independent has its positives," she said, chin up and out. "Self-sufficiency is a good thing when it helps you realize you can handle anything that comes your way."

"True," he said. "Of course, you're preaching to the choir on the praises of not needing anyone."

She smiled and it lit up her face. The connection he felt to her returned. Kindred spirits?

"I guess I am," she said as she looked around. "So, let me help you get back to yours."

She made a good argument. He wanted nothing more than to heal fast and get back to his life—a life that somehow felt a little more empty when he thought about it. Not ever needing anyone also meant coming home to an empty house every night. The timing of the thought wasn't lost on him, considering he liked having Naomi here more than he wanted to admit. She fit in ways he didn't even realize were broken.

Harding chalked his sentiment up to being stuck on his backside since being shot. Having spent the morning alone with no one to talk to after Barrett left struck Harding in a strange place. For a split-second, his mind had snapped to his future self in thirty years when he was too old to work in his current field and too young for the grave, plus all those years in between. The thought had never made his life feel empty until now, until Naomi.

The idea of spending the rest of his life with someone he barely knew sounded pretty out there, even to him in his current state. The question wasn't really whether or not him and Naomi could make it the distance, considering they would never get the chance to try. Or, could he compete with a ghost?

——————

For Naomi's own good, she needed to ignore all the sensations bringing long-forgotten body parts to life as she made physical contact with Harding. Shifting focus, she helped him stand up and walk to the downstairs guest bedroom.

The room had another four-poster bed along with a comfortable leather chair off to one side. There was a small dresser being used as a nightstand. The color palette in the room was warm with a few masculine browns, like in the leather chair.

"Your home is beautiful, by the way," Naomi said as she deposited Harding at the bathroom door.

"I had help," he said and qualified the comment with, "Marianne worked at Quinnland for my uncle. The two are now married and she was like a second mother to me while growing up. She insisted on helping decorate when I bought this place a few years ago. I trusted her taste and gave her free reign. She did an amazing job, just like I knew she would. Besides, me and decorating? My home would have ended up looking like a frat house, considering I have no clue how to make a place into a real home."

"Did you pick out the art and the furniture?" she asked, figuring he wasn't giving himself nearly enough credit. Besides, she already knew the answer to the question before she'd asked it. There was no way a man like Harding would just hand over the keys to his personal space. He had to have had a big hand in the end result.

"Yes, but Marianne weeded through a whole lot of the choices for me first," he admitted.

"Because this place is too much of you for you not to have been involved," she said. Her comment brought a wide smile and she could swear his chest puffed out a little.

"Thank you," he said. "I'll take that as a compliment."

"Believe me, it is," she reassured. A little part of her was grateful the decorations didn't happen during a past relationship. She brought her hand up to finger the lettering on the dog tags as a twinge of guilt stabbed her in the center of the chest. "These belonged to my high school boyfriend. His name was Gavin."

Harding stopped and turned. His gaze caught hers and lingered. In that moment, it was like her mind was suddenly stripped bare and he could read her thoughts.

"I'm sorry," he said low. Those two words spoken from his lips broke up some of the weight that had been sitting on her chest, making it hard to breathe since the day she got the news about Gavin.

"We were high school sweethearts who broke up and then reconnected a couple of years ago. It was like no time had passed at all and we slipped right back into our relationship," she said. Hearing those words spoken out loud, it struck her just how much dating Gavin again had felt like slipping into something comfortable, like curling up in her favorite chair. There'd been ease and history, but what about fireworks?

Naomi could be honest with herself. There hadn't been any. In high school, there'd been a crush. Looking back, it was probably nothing more than puppy love despite how real and grown-up it had felt at the time.

"It must have been even harder to lose someone you cared about twice in one lifetime," he soothed. His voice smoothed over her body and inside her heart, wrapping her in the warmth.

A well of emotion sprung, catching her off guard. Moisture gathered in her eyes. She ducked her head, chin to chest, to hide her reaction to speaking about Gavin.

Harding's hand came up to her chin and lifted her face until their eyes met.

"You don't have to be ashamed about loving someone so much that losing them brings tears to your eyes," he said, and there was so much understanding in his voice. She wanted to lean into it, into him, and get lost for a while.

"Why are you so understanding?" she asked, wondering if he'd lost someone important to him too.

He gave a slight headshake that revealed more than words ever could. Her suspicion was confirmed.

"It was forever ago," he said quietly. "And you know what they say, time heals all wounds."

"What happened?" she couldn't help but ask.

"Car crash on the highway," he said before adding, "on her way to see me after a fight."

Maybe the intense attraction brewing between them was nothing more or less than two damaged hearts recognizing a kindred spirit.

"Did you love her?" Naomi asked, wishing she could take the question back as she heard it out loud.

"At the time, I believed I did. We were young," he explained. "Didn't know any different."

"How many real relationships have you had since then?" she asked, letting curiosity get the best of her.

"Serious ones?" Harding stood there for a long moment in silence. Then came, "None."

It was her turn to nod.

"Which doesn't mean that I haven't dated around," he clarified.

"No one could replace her, right?" she asked.

"I guess not," he said after a thoughtful pause. "But I think it has more to do with the fact she's gone and I never felt like I deserved to be the one to live."

Was that the reason he put his life on the line every day?

Still, the feeling was familiar.

"Gavin lost his life protecting our freedoms and our way of life," she said. "I think about his sacrifice a lot."

"You said he came back into your life..."

She nodded.

"Were you planning a future together?" he asked.

"Yes," she admitted. Normally, she couldn't mention Gavin's name to anyone else, let alone someone she hadn't even known for a whole week yet.

"And now you'll never know how the relationship

would have played out, because he's gone," Harding surmised. He was right on point.

"I'm guessing you know this because you've been through something similar," she stated.

"You and I belong to a very small club," he said. "It's not one I'd wish on my worst enemy."

She wouldn't argue there.

"Can I ask another question?" he continued.

"Of course," she said without hesitation. The dam had been broken and she found that she suddenly wanted to talk about Gavin, about the loss. For the first time since losing him, she actually wanted to open up to someone about her former friend and fiancé. After all, it had been their bond that made them connect the second time around even if the fireworks weren't there. Their shared history and deep affection toward one another was more than most couples ever got.

"If you could go back in time, would you do it all over again?" he asked, taking a step toward her and closing the gap between them.

The question caught her off guard, and stumped her at the same time.

"I guess I don't have an answer," she said, dumbfounded.

In that moment, with Harding standing within inches of her, all she could think about was bringing her hands to loop around his neck. Her next move wasn't planned. She pressed up to her tiptoes and kissed him.

CHAPTER ELEVEN

The minute Naomi's lips touched his, Harding was in trouble. Powerless to stop the tsunami building inside him, threatening to unleash a massive tide, all he could do was surrender. Would they be swept in or away by the all-consuming tidal wave?

This wasn't the time to be rational. Harding had never considered himself an emotional person, so the fact that his emotions had grabbed the wheel and pushed all logic to the side knocked him off balance. He'd never wanted something so much as he wanted Naomi's lips against his.

She parted hers and teased his tongue inside her mouth. One thing was certain. His dark roast coffee tasted a whole lot better on her lips than in any cup.

It would be so easy to stand here and get lost in the kiss. But should they?

Harding had never debated whether or not it was a good idea to kiss someone before. When he knew, he knew. This was different. This kiss was different. Naomi was different.

Holding her, kissing her, was a game-changer like nothing he'd ever experienced. The rightness of looping his arms around her waist and pulling her closer to his body was beyond description.

Before he let this moment go any further, he needed to know that she was over losing Gavin. Drawing on all the willpower he had left inside him, Harding pulled back.

"I want this to happen," he said and could hear the huskiness in his own voice. "More than you could ever know."

"But?"

He leaned forward until his forehead rested on hers. Their breath was quick and their chests heaved for more oxygen.

"I can't be a substitution for the person you want to belong to," he said. The words might be sincere but they caught him off guard just the same.

"What are you saying?" she asked.

"That as long as you wear those, you belong to someone else." He brought his finger up to the chain and tugged at it. The dog tags jingled as they smacked into one another. "All I can say is that he's one helluva lucky man to be loved by you."

"I'm sorry for kissing you," she said, clearing her throat and then taking in a deep breath. "That was out of line."

"There's no need to apologize. You might have been the one to act but that didn't mean I wanted it to happen any less than you did," he said, hiding the disappointment causing an ache in his chest.

He'd let go of Trinity years ago. Losing her at twenty-five when he'd thought he had the world all figured out had been soul crushing. With age came the realization that he'd been infatuated with her. They'd only known each other a couple of months when the accident had happened, and there'd already been signs a breakup was pending. Take the fight, for instance. They'd gotten into it because she'd met her ex-boyfriend for dinner the night before. Going behind his back to meet her ex wasn't saying a whole lot about their trust but he wouldn't necessarily have ended the relationship over it. The fight came about because she'd lied and said she would be with her mother. Lying about seeing an ex was a sure sign that a relationship was at the beginning of the end. Trinity hadn't been ready to agree, so she decided to come show him how much he meant to her. Regret filled him at the senseless loss of life from the accident and the inability to trust that had plagued him ever since her betrayal.

Every relationship after, he hit a wall when it came time to truly open his heart. He'd buried the ability along with Trinity and had never looked back...until now. Until Naomi. All of a sudden, he found himself opening up to her, trusting her.

"It probably shouldn't happen again," Naomi said as her gaze searched his.

"Probably not," he agreed. Although, nothing about their pact felt right to him. For the moment, he would step away and grab a shower. Put a wall between them so he could refocus his energy on the case. She'd made a good point earlier about getting some rest in order to speed up the healing process. A good night of sleep might be just what he needed. Overthinking a case didn't always yield the results he wanted. Sometimes, it was better to step away and let the answers come to him.

Besides, if he stood here any longer the temptation to kiss Naomi might cause him to do something he would regret.

"I'll be right here if you need anything," she said as he turned and walked through the door. He closed it behind him, not reacting to her statement because he wanted to tell her that he needed her. They couldn't possibly know each other well enough for the emotions claiming him. Those tried to convince him Naomi was the kind of person who came along once in a lifetime. This might be a case of right people, wrong time. It was possible that in a year or two she might come to terms with losing Gavin. Now that Dog Tags had a name, he became that much more real.

Gavin's memory would hold Naomi back from moving on. He didn't want to think about how much that made his heart ache.

The downstairs shower was a bathtub combo. Harding sat on the edge of the tub before turning on the spigot. Getting undressed was the tricky part. Standing at the sink helped a great deal. His thoughts drifted back to the two-word message: *Go home.*

There were more black trucks in Texas than armadillos, or so it seemed. The statement was probably an exaggeration, but it did little to narrow the field. Exactly the reason the driver felt comfortable using the truck, Harding figured. A vehicle that would blend right in made for an easy getaway. The driver could disappear onto a highway.

Wincing as he bent over to slip his jeans off, Harding knew his injuries were worse than he wanted to admit. It put him at a disadvantage when it came to helping Naomi, which he very much wanted to do. The other handicap came in the form of not being able to use resources from work. It would be unethical to tap into any of the databases there for an under-the-radar case. Him working on it during his time off was fine.

Stepping out of his jeans and into the shower, Harding considered the primary suspects. He had yet to get on his laptop to investigate the dating app men, so he would focus on the people at her work while he soaped himself as best as he could. Washing his hair forced him to lift his arms higher than they wanted to go. He moved slowly so he wouldn't rip any stitches out. The last thing he needed was a trip back to the ER. Naomi would insist if she found out and if they were going to get along there couldn't be any secrets between them, not when it came to his healing.

Toweling off was tricky, but he managed. He was determined to dress himself too. Boxers and a cotton t-shirt were the best he could manage and would cover all the important parts. He got the boxers on before opening the door to ask for help removing the cling wrap.

Naomi stood up the second the door opened. She bit back a yawn as she made a beeline for him.

"Everything okay?" she asked. Her forehead creased

with concern, so he must have been making a face without realizing it.

"All good," he said. "I could use some help taking off the Saran Wrap so I can finish washing. A shower felt pretty great."

"Nice to be clean, isn't it?" she said as she followed him back into the bathroom. "I always try to get my patients into a shower as quickly as possible. There's something magic about something so basic as being clean after someone's been in an accident or had emergency surgery, like in your case."

"I guess you could say I had both," he said, noticing she didn't look at him when she talked about how he'd gotten his injury. Did she have a hang-up about him being shot? "I'm not normally in the habit of jumping in front of bullets, but a fragment got me."

"A job like yours could bring a whole lot of devastation to loved ones on any shift," she said, before rushing to apologize.

Now, he had two strikes. The first, he figured, was the fact her boyfriend was gone. It dawned on Harding that Gavin was most likely killed in the line of duty. Had he been shot as well? So, she was still hung up on Gavin. Strike one. Plenty of single folks refused to date cops, firefighters, and others who worked in law enforcement. Call it a job hazard, but it was one every person in said jobs had come across during the course of their career. And her late boyfriend had worked in a dangerous job being in the military. Harding worked in a dangerous job. Strike two.

An image was beginning to form as to why a wall seemed to come up between them every time they got close. He didn't need to be a crack investigator to put two-and-two together.

Shame, he thought. He could have really liked Naomi, and he could count on one finger how many times he could say that about someone he'd known as short a time as they had. Gut instinct said she was someone special and could be important in his life. With two strikes against him, they'd be lucky to call each other a friend when the case was over. He had a feeling she wasn't the brunch and coffee meetup type. To be honest, neither was he and once his injuries healed enough to allow him to go back to work, he'd be back on the job in a heartbeat.

So, why did that suddenly seem less than appealing?

———

"Are your washrags in here?" Naomi asked as she motioned toward the cabinet.

"Yes, on the top shelf," Harding said, and his voice was low, gravelly. He stood there with water dripping down his muscled chest and she'd had to force her gaze away or be too tempted to touch him again.

Touching Harding was one of those bad ideas that seemed oh-so-right in the moment. Like eating a pint of chocolate mint ice cream while watching a movie right before bed. Sure, it felt good in the moment, but the sugar rush would ensure she couldn't sleep and her stomach would be unsettled for the rest of the evening if she polished off the whole container.

Except that kissing him had had no such backlash to

date. Not to mention the man's abs made a washboard look lazy.

Naomi forced his insanely in-shape body out of her thoughts. It would probably help if she wasn't in a tight space with him where every time she inhaled air she ushered in his clean and masculine scent. He smelled like a cedarwood candle wrapped in a big bow of sex appeal.

Working the washrag in the sink with a bar of soap helped ease some of the tension stringing her muscles taut. The kiss a little while ago had lasted mere seconds and yet left a mark on her that would last a lifetime. No kiss could compare to Harding's and he'd been containing himself, unlike her.

Naomi could blame it on the stress of her last shift or lack of sleep, but she'd been clear-minded when she'd pushed up to her tiptoes and planted a kiss on those thick lips of his. The man's steel-colored eyes were hooded by the thickest, blackest set of lashes she'd ever seen. The way they highlighted his eyes should be against the law.

Taking in a fortifying breath, she rubbed the bar on the washcloth a little harder. When she was certain there was enough soap, she pulled another washcloth out of the cabinet, held it under the sink and then handed it over. First the wet cloth. Then the soapy one followed by a fresh wet cloth.

"Can you get my back?" he asked, turning around like he hadn't just asked her to touch his strong back.

"Sure," she managed to croak out. Her throat was suddenly so dry it felt like she'd just licked a glue stick. Her tongue felt like she'd just eaten wallpaper paste.

And her pulse raced. Being in this bathroom with Harding felt strangely intimate despite just doing her job like she'd done dozens of times before. She'd actually helped patients wash off when they couldn't get out of bed, so this should be no different.

This seemed like a good time to remind herself Harding worked as a U.S. Marshal. His job meant that he might not come home every night. Despite the enormous respect she had for those who served their communities and country, dating after Gavin was too far out of her comfort zone.

She made quick but thorough work of cleaning Harding's back, knowing how good he would feel to be all clean. She'd heard from patients time and time again how a shower helped them get a better night of sleep, and she hoped it would be the case with Harding.

Besides, one day was almost down. Two to go. She could do anything for two days. That was only, like, forty-eight hours. Anything but stop herself from falling for Harding, she feared.

"All done," she said before rinsing all the washcloths off and spreading them across the shower rod to dry. She turned in time to see Harding struggling with getting his white cotton t-shirt on. "Here, let me help with that."

He stopped fighting with the shirt but his expression was one of deep frustration.

"I can't imagine how difficult this must be for someone so used to doing everything for himself," she started as she took one end of the shirt and helped stretch the collar over his head. He got one arm in with a serious wince. She slowly stretched out the shirt until he could shrug his other arm into it.

"Better," he said, and she noticed he didn't respond to her comment.

"Let's get you to bed," she said.

"Promises, promises," he said so low she barely heard him. His face broke into a dry crack of a smile. When she didn't respond, he added, "Come on. That was funny. Tell me you want to laugh and are holding back."

"I do when a joke is original," she said with a straight face as she guided his arm around her shoulders for support. She looked up at him, made eye contact, and then broke into a smile. "Got you."

"You sure do." He seemed to realize the mistake quickly when he corrected himself. "Did."

"I used to laugh a whole lot more," she said, ignoring the slip. But was her statement really true? She'd worked to put herself through nursing school. She'd worked her behind off to prove she could do a good job. When she looked back at the past decade of her life, laughing wasn't exactly something she remembered doing much of. Working? Yes. Fun? Not so much. "Or maybe I should say that I plan to laugh more in the future. That would probably be more honest."

"Deal," he said without missing a beat like he intended to be there to participate. If only she could let him.

After helping him to bed, she ran upstairs to brush her teeth and wash her face. She came back down and walked into the guestroom as he turned down the lights.

"What are you doing here?" he asked.

"Sleeping in the chair. Where's an extra blanket?" she asked.

"You can't sleep in a chair," he said. He seemed to quickly recover from the initial shock of her coming back into the room. "Plus, I can manage on my own for a few hours."

"What if you need me in the middle of the night?" she asked. "I'll never hear you from the second floor. Plus, believe me, I can sleep anywhere if I have a reasonably dark room. The fact that I had a chance to wash my face and brush my teeth is a dream."

Harding stared at her for a long moment and for a split-second she thought he might order her to leave the room. Instead, he opened the covers.

"Climb in. We can put a pillow in between us if it'll make you more comfortable sleeping here," he said.

The bed was large enough to accommodate both of them, despite his considerable size. The question was whether or not it was a good idea for her heart. Being close to Harding gave her a sense of calm like she'd never known. Which was strange when she really thought about it because he also awakened all her senses.

"Come on," he urged. "I promise not to bite."

Shame, she thought, before taking him up on his offer. Mistake or not, Naomi was too tired to argue. And, besides, her heart couldn't refuse.

She climbed into bed and under the covers, her body a mix of sensual shivers skittering across her skin and warmth circling low in her belly as she curled up next to him. How could she not be super aware of the strong male presence lying next to her as she breathed in his spicy scent? Harding was perfect and she wanted nothing more than to be able to open her heart to him. Could she go there with him? Or would guilt and regret stop her?

CHAPTER TWELVE

Harding woke with a start. The sound of his front door opening caused him to throw the covers off and reach for the nightstand where he kept a Sig Sauer for protection.

"Hello?" Barrett called out from the living room. "Harding?"

Naomi sat up and gasped. Harding could see how this might look to his brother. Barrett wouldn't care, by the way, but Naomi seemed embarrassed being caught in bed with her patient.

"I'll handle this," he whispered to her before forcing himself to get out of bed, despite how much his body wanted to stay put. Pain screamed at him from the right side where his rib was bruised. He managed to throw on a pair of jeans before returning his weapon to the nightstand.

Walking into the next room took herculean effort, but he made it.

"Hey," he said to Barrett. "What are you doing here this morning?"

"Stopped by before work to check on my brother after he told me not to bother yesterday. Or is that suddenly not okay?" Barrett's forehead creased with confusion.

"It's fine," Harding said, shrugging it off like his reaction wasn't at all over the top. He saw a bag in his brother's hand that looked like it came from his favorite bagel shop and this seemed like a real good time to change the subject. "What are you holding there?"

Barrett walked directly past Harding and into the kitchen where he set down the bag of bagels on top of the marble island.

"I felt sorry for you after seeing the condition you were in when I left yesterday," Barrett started, getting out two plates from the cabinet. "Coffee?"

"No, thanks," Harding stated.

His brother shot him another look.

"Mind if I make a pot?" Barrett asked.

"Go ahead," Harding said, trying to play it cool.

"I didn't see a vehicle parked out front, so I'm guessing your 'super nurse' got sick of you and went home last night. You should have called. I could have slept over and gone to work from here." Barrett froze the second he turned around. His gaze fixed at a spot to the left of Harding's shoulder.

Harding mouthed the words, "Super nurse?"

"Yeah, my bad," Barrett admitted before practically falling all over himself by way of apology.

"Don't worry about it," Naomi played it off like it was nothing. "I always sleep in my patient's room when

I take a homecare gig, in case they fall in the middle of the night and need help."

"True," Harding said quickly. A little too quickly? Based on Barrett's raised eyebrow the answer was a resounding yes.

"I brought bagels," Barrett said. His brother seemed content to leave it alone and that was fine by Harding. The two had a habit of teasing each other, but the subject of Naomi needed to be off limits.

"My favorite," she said. "Is that coffee brewing?"

Barrett broke into a wide smile.

"Let me run upstairs to freshen up and I'll take one of those bagels," she said before disappearing.

Barrett stood there for a long moment like he was about to mind his own business. Then, he smiled. "I knew there was something different about you this morning. You look...too well rested."

"Funny," Harding said in an attempt to quash the conversation right there.

"Now, I know why," he said, motioning toward the stairs.

"Leave it alone," Harding warned, surprised by the ire in his own town. "Let's just keep this subject out of bounds for now. Okay, bro?"

"Fine by me," Barrett said, pretending to not be phased in the least. "I just came for the free coffee."

"Then, go ahead and fix one for me too," Harding conceded, realizing his brother planned to stick around.

He fixed three cups as Harding took a seat at the island.

"All kidding aside, you look a helluva lot better this morning," Barrett said, and Harding could see the relief in his brother's eyes. If the shoe were on the other foot, he'd be concerned about his brother.

"I slept for a solid ten hours," Harding admitted. He couldn't remember the last time he'd gotten that much rest. "Turns out, sleep does wonders for bullet holes."

"Sleep is good," Barrett parroted, distracted. He started to say something but seemed to think better of it when he clamped his mouth shut. The timing couldn't have been better because Naomi came bopping down the stairs before starting toward the coffee machine.

"Already poured," Barrett said to her. He motioned toward the stool beside Harding. "Sit. I'm sure this guy worked you to death yesterday, so I'll take care of you both for breakfast. How does that sound?"

"Like I'm about to be spoiled," she quipped with the kind of smile that could shed light on the darkest room.

Harding couldn't remember the last time he'd slept a solid night let alone ten hours. His muscles were warming up now after being stiff. He had two days left to make progress on the investigation before Naomi went back to her job at the hospital. Was it unsafe to return?

"I'm about to head to work," Barrett said before turning his attention to Naomi, who'd just reclaimed her seat. "Thank you for helping my brother. I'm not sure what we would have done without you since he's too stubborn to let any of us take a day off."

"Speaking of which, do you mind updating the family? Let them know I have full-time care for the next couple of days while I get back on my feet?" he asked Barrett.

"Not at all," he responded. "I'll do it once I get to work."

"Thank you," Harding said to his brother, forcing himself to stand up and walk around the marble island for a bear hug. Lifting his arms hurt. Moving hurt. But the pain was worth it in order to properly thank his brother. Being around Naomi made him realize how fortunate he was to have so many people in his life who cared about him. People he'd taken for granted. Well, not anymore. "I appreciate everything you've done and are doing for me."

"Goes without saying, bro," Barrett responded, tightening their hug before a quick release. "I don't want to hurt you."

"It would take bigger muscles than those measly things to do real damage," Harding quipped, brightening the tone.

Barrett laughed and so did Naomi.

"That's my cue to head out," Barrett said. "But I'm a nice guy so I'll leave the bagels behind."

"I doubt you'd get out the door if you tried to take them with you," Naomi said with a smile as she wiggled her eyebrows. Having her get along with Barrett so well flooded Harding's heart with more of that light.

"Another tough guy, huh?" Barrett didn't miss a beat.

"Looks like it," she said, picking a bagel out of the bag before smothering it in cream cheese. She took a bite and a little mewl of pleasure escaped. "This really is heaven."

Barrett's chest puffed out a little bit more.

"Yep," he said as he downed the contents of his

coffee mug. He rinsed out the cup and set it in the sink. "Enjoy the rest."

"We will," Harding said.

"I'll check in with you later," Barrett said.

"Sounds like a plan." Harding responded. "You know the way out. Do you mind locking the door?"

The last comment elicited a raised eyebrow from Barrett, but he seemed content to let it slide without addressing it. Yes, it was an unusual request while Harding was home. And, no, he couldn't explain to his brother without involving him, so he hadn't updated Barrett on it.

The details of the investigation weren't the only card Harding held close to his chest. His growing feelings for the auburn beauty with intense violet eyes could interfere with his judgment. Being an objective investigator made him good at his job. The only course of action when it came to personal feelings toward Naomi was to try to forget the kiss had ever happened no matter how much his heart begged for more.

———

"Now that you have something in your stomach, how about some ibuprofen?" Naomi shoved the rightness of being in the kitchen and joking around down somewhere deep. Burying her feelings was the best and only choice.

"Couldn't hurt," Harding said as he polished off the last of his everything bagel.

"I had no idea breakfast could taste so good," Naomi said as she retrieved the pills. She emptied four onto her palm and then brought them over to Harding. "And you'll have to tell me where you bought that mattress, because I haven't slept this well in too long."

A look passed behind Harding's eyes that said maybe it wasn't the mattress. She wouldn't touch that thought. Sleeping with him in the same bed had given her comfort when she hadn't slept well in far too long.

"What's on the agenda today?" she asked as she handed over a glass of water.

Harding dry-swallowed the pills before taking a sip. He set the glass down.

"I'd like to see how much movement I can get out this body," he started, "as we continue working on the case, of course."

"You didn't talk about my 'situation' with your brother today, I noticed," she said.

"Figured it was best to leave it alone for now. Besides, he would want to see it through," he stated.

"Quinn family trait?" she asked.

"Afraid so." He nodded.

For the second time in less than twenty-four hours she thought there should be more Quinns in the world. Hands down, it would be a better place. One where people's word could be counted on. Justice would rule, she was certain of that. And there would be a whole lot more kindness. She was beginning to realize Harding had offered this job to her for more reasons than one. He needed help, but he was already up and around better than anyone should be in his condition. Being physically fit helped so much in healing injuries. His main motivation seemed to be the fact he had something to offer her. She had a problem, and he was more eager to talk about her than the steps to his recovery.

"How are you feeling today?" she asked, redirecting the conversation.

"I've been better," he said.

"Scale of one to ten, what is your pain level today?" she continued.

"I'd say a four right now, and once the ibuprofen kicks in I'm probably looking at a two or three," he admitted.

"Amazing," she said before clearing the mess on the marble island.

"I'm a fast healer," he said.

"I can see that," she stated. "You're doing great. I'd like to redress the stitches and see what the incision area looks like today. We washed it last night but it wouldn't hurt to add some antibiotic ointment today."

It didn't take long to clean up and do the dishes. She stretched her arms out, thinking she hadn't felt this good in a while. A good night of sleep seemed to hit the reset button on her stress levels too. Funny because she knew getting good sleep, eating well, and getting enough exercise was the recipe for feeling good in theory. In practice, errands had to be run, life got busy, and eating on the go happened.

"Sounds like a plan," he said. He pushed up to standing with some effort, and then retrieved the familiar sheet of paper. He located a pen and then reclaimed his seat after refilling his coffee mug.

"You're moving around great," she said in awe. "I'm not sure you'll need me all three days at this rate."

"Stick around anyway," he said, lifting the pad of

paper. "It'll give us time to work, and I could use the company."

"Okay," she said, realizing how much she actually wanted to be here. His place was cozy and comfortable, and she felt right at home.

"I have Theo, and Sara written down from your work so far," Harding started before taking a sip of coffee. "Has anyone else asked you out?"

"I mean, not really, no one that I said yes to," she said.

Harding's forehead creased in what looked like serious concentration. "I'm not as interested in the people you said yes to, as much as the folks you turned down," he said. "Or anyone who hinted they'd like to date you. Or a conversation that stands out in your mind as weird or threw you off in some way."

"Now that I really think about it, I had a strange conversation with Dr. Juno during my last shift," she said on a sigh. "He asked me to call him by his first name a few months ago, but I told that it didn't seem right or feel professional. He's been looking out for me, and he hinted that he wouldn't mind dating a while ago. I wouldn't say that he has ever asked me out specifically."

"Explain what, 'specifically' means to you," he continued.

"There have been a few times when he asked what I was doing on my day off and when I gave my laundry list of not exciting activities, he backed off the topic." This line of thinking was bringing back a couple of uncomfortable conversations the two of them had had.

"Sounds like he can be protective of you," Harding

surmised. The way his eyebrow shot up as he spoke made a few more instances click.

"When he was new, he used to hang around the nurse's station a lot on my shift," she recalled. "Rita used to joke that my boyfriend was behind me, but she would say it so low he couldn't hear. She makes jokes like that about others too. She was on Theo at one point because he always gets extra nervous when he speaks to me. She was convinced he had a crush on me for a while."

"And you? What do you think?" he asked.

"That he gets nervous speaking to anyone he has a crush on," she said. "I highly doubt I'm the only person at the hospital he sees that way. I've overheard others say not-so-nice things about him behind his back. He really is a kind soul though. I would have said he didn't have a mean bone in his body until last night."

"And protective," he said, circling Theo's name while adding Dr. Juno to the list. "What about this Rod character? Has he ever asked you out?"

"Rod? No," she said quickly. "The only thing he ever did was make me feel like I was being paranoid. The so-called gifts left on my vehicle were supposed to be compliments in his words. The silk robe was a little bit too personal if you ask me."

"Silk robe?" he parroted. "You didn't tell me about that one before. That is very personal."

"I thought I did," she said, realizing she'd been so stressed it probably wasn't the only thing she was forgetting to mention.

In a surprise move, Harding added Rod's name to the list.

"Really?" she asked. "You think..."

"I don't know, which is why his name goes here," he said. "Sometimes, the person behind a crime is the one positioning himself or herself as the least likely candidate. It's the same reason killers show up in search parties to help find victims when they know exactly what happened. They get a thrill out of being involved right under law enforcement's nose."

"Sounds twisted," she said.

"It is," he quickly added. "And more common than you'd think."

"Then, Rod goes on the list," she said with a shiver. "It creeps me out that I went to him for help if he's the one behind the whole thing."

"It's understandable. For now, he's suspect. We follow wherever the evidence leads," Harding said, and it sounded logical.

The whole situation was creepy, though.

"Tell me about your dating experiences," he said. "We'll start with Mario."

She cleared her throat and tried to shake off the awkwardness that accompanied talking specifically about her dating life with Harding. Then again, maybe that was exactly what she needed to do. Remind herself the two of them weren't dating and try to forget the kiss from last night that would now be the benchmark for the future.

"Mario was pushy," she said. "I wanted to meet for coffee and he tried to switch to a bar. Said he was more relaxed if he was able to sit down and have a drink. I nixed the idea and then canceled the date. He got heated about it, so I figured he was the last guy I wanted to spend fifteen minutes with, let alone an hour, coffee shop or otherwise."

"So, you never met up?" Harding asked.

"Nope. He was out pretty quick," she said. "The only reason I brought him up is because I made the mistake of giving him my cell phone number and he texted me a couple of times trying to force the date. I eventually blocked him but not before he sent a message telling me that I'd be sorry and that I was missing out."

Harding issued a grunt.

"Mario sounds like a real winner," he said. A mix of emotion passed behind his eyes that she couldn't quite pinpoint. It was probably wrong of her to want to see jealousy there. She'd never felt so much fire and promise than when she was in the same room with Harding.

Hers and Gavin's relationship had been sweet. They'd been close friends and, in high school, she'd been able to tell him most everything. The military had changed him, hardened him a little around the edges, but she could see the kindhearted Gavin still in there and figured he would return once he left the military for civilian life. Fireworks could best describe the feeling in her chest when she was with Harding. Her feelings for him could easily run out of control, like an unbridled wildfire.

"Exactly the reason there was no date," she said, forcing thoughts about her feelings for Harding from her mind.

"Did you report him to the dating site?" he asked.

"I should have, but, honestly, I didn't think about it at the time," she admitted. "Rita had talked me into swiping four others. When I told her that Mario turned out to be a jerk, she rolled her eyes and said it was time to move on. Said she'd kissed a few frogs online too just like in real life."

The look on Harding's face said he didn't like this one bit.

CHAPTER THIRTEEN

"I don't like Mario's attitude but I'm not sure he would go to the lengths this stalker has when the two of you didn't meet in person," Harding reasoned. In a typical stalking case, the victim knew the stalker. It was the reason he kept circling back to the people she worked with, but every avenue needed to be explored.

"That's fair," Naomi said.

"The next name on the list is Raul," he said, and he could swear her face muscles tensed at hearing the name.

"Raul seemed like a nice guy," she explained. "He wasn't my type, and I knew it right away. We made it to coffee, but I had a panic attack and had to get out of there for air. I quickly excused myself, made up a bogus reason like a sudden stomachache, and I never heard from him again."

"He would have seen your vehicle," Harding said, thinking Mario wouldn't have known what she drove or where she worked.

"True," she said. "I must have hurt his feelings even though I apologized with a direct message on the dating app. I felt like I owed him a better explanation so I admitted that I wasn't over my ex yet. It was kind of true, when you really think about it. I just didn't share the whole tragic story about Gavin being dead."

"How did this guy respond?" Harding tapped the end of the pen against the marble.

"There was cursing," she recalled. "At me. He said I shouldn't be on a site if I wasn't ready to date." She shrugged. "What could I say except that I agreed with him."

"He still sounds like a jerk. How is someone supposed to know if they're ready to move on unless they try?" he stated, figuring she'd done the right thing by testing the waters.

"I agree with you in theory, but I wasn't ready for any of it. Rita pushed me into the whole thing, and I naively thought it would be easier to get back in the swing of things than it turned out to be," she said on a sigh.

"Raul sounds bitter, but again, there doesn't seem to be a solid reason for him to show up at your work and leave things on your vehicle," he said, and the more he reasoned it out, the worse it looked like she felt. Because signs were pointing to someone at work being responsible. She involuntarily shivered and it was all he could do not to reach out to comfort her.

"Steven and I made it to a second date," she continued, pushing ahead despite looking like she'd rather eat worms than keep going. Harding didn't exactly love hearing about her dates, but this was important and he was trained to set his personal feelings aside. Normally, that wasn't a problem. "I let him pick me up from my house. According to Rita, dinner was an official date. He parked and walked me to the door after a decent meal. I didn't have a connection to him but I didn't want to jump up and run out the door after sitting down for five minutes. I thought I was making progress, whereas he interpreted the date differently."

"He thought you were into him?" Harding asked, ignoring the hollow in his chest that came with fighting the urge to hold her.

"It would seem so," she said. "He went for a kiss. I ducked out of the way and then thanked him for the evening. He basically told me that he'd dropped a lot of money on dinner, and that he liked me. In so many words, he said I 'owed' him something for shelling out a hundred bucks for food."

"The Stevens of the world give the rest of us a bad name," Harding muttered along with another grunt.

"He was persistent. Made an excuse about needing to use my bathroom before making a long drive home," she stated.

"What did you do?" he asked, realizing he'd fisted his hands. Harding flexed and released his fingers a couple of times to work off the tension.

"I unlocked the door and then told him I'd be waiting outside for him," she said. "He decided he could hold it for the ride home when I sat down on the step of my porch."

"Did he try to contact you afterward?" he asked, figuring this guy might be more than a jerk.

"Not for two weeks," she said. "Then, he texted

saying he'd had a good time, his nerves had gotten the best of him, and that he promised to be better if I gave him a second chance. He said he'd been in a bad relationship that had ended and had been struggling ever since."

"Did you? Give him a second chance?" he asked, hoping he already knew the answer.

"No," she said as relief flooded Harding. "If that was the first impression he made, I didn't see how a repeat would be any better. Besides, I told him that I thought he should take some time to get over his ex before he tried to date again."

"I'm guessing that went over about as well as hot sauce on an ice cream sundae," he stated. A guy who felt entitled to something from a woman for the simple act of paying for dinner wasn't just a person without class. He might be dangerous. If she'd allowed him inside her apartment, he seemed the type to force himself on someone. He didn't seem like he understood that no truly meant no. Harding would like five minutes alone with him, or any other guy who shared that mentality, to make sure they understood what would happen to themselves if they ever raped a woman.

"You would be right," she said as he drew a circle around Steven's name.

"That leaves Kevin and Knox," he stated.

"Kevin was a bust. Didn't make it past the coffee screening date," she admitted. "Kevin kept checking his watch during the date. Apparently, he had another date lined up who got the times mixed up and showed up during our meetup. At that point, I canceled the date with Knox. I couldn't keep going. Told him I needed a break, and he didn't take it well. In fact, he ended the call while I was still midsentence after muttering a word that I probably shouldn't repeat."

Another shot of anger ripped through him. What did these men hope to gain by being absolute jerks?

Although Harding had enjoyed playing the field for a number of years, his own recent dating history had felt incredibly lacking. Lacking what? There was the problem. He'd dated everything from waitresses to lawyers and yet couldn't seem to find a real spark with any of them and nothing compared to the one he felt with Naomi. In the past year or so, it felt like every date was basically the same with very little difference in the person sitting across the dinner table from him. Finding a connection, like the one he felt with Naomi from the moment she walked into his hospital room, had been something he'd all but given up on.

At least now he knew it existed. That was probably a good thing. The downside? Naomi didn't seem to feel the same way. And that was a real bummer because his lips still tingled with heat from the fireworks in the kiss they'd shared.

———

Thinking back on Naomi's recent dates, there wasn't one person she had wanted to get close to, let alone kiss like she'd boldly done last night with Harding. She was beginning to think she'd found the right person at the wrong time. Of course, wasn't that the story of her life?

When her and Gavin had been young and in love, the timing had been bad. They'd needed to experience life and grow up before settling into a real long-term relationship. After that kiss with Harding, she couldn't help but wonder if her and Gavin would have been strong enough to go the distance. Would their friendship carry them through the long haul? A little voice in the back of her mind picked that moment to point out that she would have lived her entire life without ever knowing a spark like the one she had with Harding was even possible.

How sad was that?

Her and Gavin had other things, like history. They'd spent so much time together in high school it was like she didn't know where she ended and he began. Granted, he'd been different, colder when they'd started up again. The comfort and familiarity had them slipping right back into old patterns. Good patterns.

Was it all an illusion? Gavin had changed. Would he get back to the person he'd been before his service changed him? She wouldn't have cared. She had so much respect for the sacrifices he was making. There was no doubt in her mind that he needed her and she wanted to be there for him.

Looking at it from a new lens, from a distance, had she been ready to sign up as his caretaker instead of equal partner? He never would have admitted it, but the wide-eyed innocence had been stomped out of his eyes, and replaced with a coldness that she didn't recognize. It made sense, though. There was no way he could do his job overseas while tapped into the kind of person who'd once carried a stray dog that weighed almost as much as him half a mile to the closest vet. Had being in the military changed him to the point he would never have been able to return to the person he'd been?

Naomi would never know now. Her own guilt for feeling like she'd somehow let him down, by not convincing him to leave the military, had practically swallowed her whole.

"Hey." Harding's voice broke into her revelry.

She shook her head.

"Sorry," she said without an explanation.

"If you ever want to talk to me about what's going on inside, when your eyes tell me you've checked out of this conversation, I'm here," he said with the kind of compassion that brought her back to life and made her feel like there might be some forgiveness out there for her.

"I'll keep that in mind," she said, and meant every word. Could she talk to him in-depth about Gavin?

"No judgment either," he said. "Whatever you tell me will always be held in strictest confidence."

Naomi had always seen wearing Gavin's dog tags as a way to honor him. But had they also become a way to ward off the world? She hadn't thought about it in this light, but they hung around her neck in an obvious place. It would be impossible to miss the chain around her neck. The message they sent was probably loud and clear to anyone who was paying attention. Did that include Harding?

She wanted to get to know him better and surprised herself in the knowledge she wanted to tell him more about her past. The only way to truly get to know each other would be to break down the walls she'd constructed around her heart. Could she?

The overwhelming desire to see if a second kiss had the same effect as the first told her that she wasn't ready to open up to Harding or anyone else. But if she was...it would be him.

"We should talk about the other names on the list," she said, wishing it was some random person she'd barely met instead of someone she had to work with day in and day out.

"I saw the way Dr. Juno looked at you at the hospital," Harding said after a long pause. He rested his elbows on the table and clasped his hands together. "I didn't like it."

Those four words shouldn't cause a trill of electricity to shoot through Naomi, especially on the heels of saying a doctor she worked closely with could be responsible for making her double-check every door lock and constantly look over her shoulder.

"What do we do now?" she asked, trying to shake it off. "What's the next step?"

"I'm going on out a limb here but anyone at the hospital would have access to surgical gloves. Lifting a print from the note might be futile," he stated. "My hands are tied in the sense that I can't use work resources and we might not get a local cop to see the note left here in the same light we do."

When he restated the facts, she didn't see a flaw in his logic.

"Asking around at work probably wouldn't do any good," she admitted. "Plus, I'm not due back for another couple of days."

"Showing up at someone's home with the note could throw them off. We might be able to tell from their reaction whether or not the person is guilty," he stated.

"I don't know where any of my co-workers live, least of all Dr. Juno," she said.

"Do you have anyone's cell number?" he asked.

"That I do have, or at least, I can get," she stated as a plan took shape. "It feels good to finally think about making my own play rather than waiting for the next thing to happen. In some ways, I'm always feeling like I'm waiting for a shoe to drop."

"You can text one person at a time, tell them you got their note, and that you'd like them to back off or you'll bring in HR," he stated.

"What about the police? Is that a better threat?" she asked.

"You could mention the law," he said. "Whichever you think would scare them the most."

"I don't think anyone wants an official report by the police on their record," she said. "Based on Rod's response when I brought this to his attention before, I'm thinking work isn't going to support me anyway. I could be wrong, but there's still a good ole boy network at play at the hospital. And a hierarchy. Plus, if there are rumors going around about me being a flirt then I won't be taken seriously."

"Unfortunately, we don't have the rose or the teddy bear either," he said.

"No. I regret not holding onto those," she stated. "It's a terrible feeling to think someone at work wants to assault my character."

The way Harding's gaze widened, she could tell an idea popped.

"There is a really good reason to discredit you when you think about it," he said and then his jaw muscle clenched.

It dawned on her what he was insinuating and made her want to vomit.

"When I lodge a real complaint or call the police, I'll have a history of crying wolf," she said.

"This person isn't counting on the fact DNA evidence will lock them behind bars for the rest of their lives," he stated.

"Unless they've done their homework and know how to avoid leaving a trail," she stated.

"True," he agreed.

This whole line of thought sent an icy chill racing down her back.

"In an actual investigation, though, home computers would be checked. There would be no hiding past searches from a skilled computer tech," he said.

"Would the person responsible for stalking me know that necessarily?" she asked.

"Potentially not," he said. "And we do generally catch those guys before they're able to act again."

Naomi retrieved her cell phone from the other room. She took a long pull off her coffee that was at room temperature by this point. And then she locked gazes with Harding. "Who do I call first?"

CHAPTER FOURTEEN

"Start with Theo," Harding advised, thinking he was the least likely to put together a complicated plan. He clearly had a crush on Naomi and was protective of her. He also wore his emotions on his sleeve and didn't strike Harding as the conniving type. And yet, evidence did point to him.

"Okay," she said. "I have to text him sometimes during work hours, so I have his number right here."

Naomi pulled up the contact and tapped on the name. She lifted her gaze to meet Harding's and his chest squeezed. Was it possible to fall for someone this fast? Because the kiss they'd shared last night put kissing at a new level. He could only imagine what it would be like to make love to Naomi, considering the heat in their kisses.

Not the time.

"Here goes," she said as the ring sounded through the speaker.

"Hello?" Theo sounded confused as to why she would be calling him.

"Hi, Theo," she started. "I hope it's okay to call you on my day off."

"Y-y-yeah, that would be f-f-fine," the young man stuttered when he spoke.

"I got your note," she said. "And I wanted to talk about it."

"M-m-my note?" Theo sounded genuinely confused. He fit the role of someone who could become obsessed with a woman he had feelings for. He wouldn't have the confidence to ask her out on a date officially. Listening to Theo now, Harding's gut instinct said Theo wasn't responsible, despite several signs that said otherwise.

"At least I thought it was from you," she continued without missing a beat.

"No," Theo protested. "I didn't write a-a-a-a note. The only th-th-thing I did was go into the patient's room like I was told to."

"Who told you to go into the patient's room?" Naomi asked.

"No one," Theo stated but it was too late to take it back now. "I didn't m-m-mean to say it."

"It's okay, Theo," Naomi said, clearly not wanting to upset him further. "I understand. No harm done." She made eyes at Harding after saying goodbye and ending the call. "Theo is being manipulated."

"Yes," Harding agreed. "To what end is anyone's guess."

"It's possible he did write the note and put it on my vehicle even though I'm almost certain he still doesn't drive. Not legally, at least," she stated. "I can ask around when I go back to work in a couple of days. The physical description of the note writer would fit half the people I know, so it isn't like I was able to narrow down the list there."

Harding hoped to have answers before Naomi returned to work. As it was, the threat was heating up and he didn't want her out of his sight without knowing who was involved or where this might lead. Escalation was always scary. Something niggled at the back of his mind, but he couldn't quite access it.

"What does Theo's mother drive?" he asked. "Do we know?"

"I'm not sure," she said.

"If we get a home address, we could always take a ride to check it out ourselves," he said.

"You shouldn't be behind the wheel, and taking my SUV is equivalent to strapping a billboard on me," she said.

"True, but you could drive my truck," he said. "I'm sure I have a ballcap around here somewhere. It wouldn't completely block your face but it would make it more difficult to identify you." She was nodding and he took it as a good sign that he was making progress with his argument.

"In fact, if we get the addresses of your co-workers, we can take the morning to do rounds," he continued, liking the idea the more he talked.

"We could do that," she said. "Mind if we check on my place while we're out? I left in such a hurry that I'm not sure I closed the window all the way in the master bedroom. It gets hot upstairs with the heater on and I leave it cracked. I think I closed and locked it, but I can't recall for certain."

"Sure," he said, figuring they could also get lunch while they were out. And, hopefully, make more progress on the case. "We can drive through the parking lot of work later tonight when the new shift begins. See who drives a black truck if we don't have any luck today."

"I'll Google the names of my co-workers and see if I can get addresses," she said before studying her phone.

It didn't take long for her eyes to light up. The sad thing was that there was no such thing as privacy any longer with the internet.

"Bingo," she said. "I got Theo's, Sara, and Dr. Juno."

"What about Rod from security?" he asked.

"I can get his too," she finally said. "I'm not sure why I never considered him as being responsible. It's too wild that he is the one I went to in order to get answers. I also asked him for more lighting in the parking lot. I mean, why wouldn't I? He is security, but still." Another shiver rocked her body, seeming to catch her off guard.

"I've seen pretty much everything in my line of work, which is why I include anyone who could remotely be involved," Harding said. Predators often worked in jobs that gave them a sense of authority over others. They liked the instant respect that came with the position and being seen as someone's 'savior.' It wasn't uncommon and he'd delivered several felony warrants personally to folks who worked in the field. Once they were caught and released, depending on the crime, they could never work in their chosen field again.

Until the first bust, though, it could provide a perfect cover. "Has he ever hinted that he liked you?"

"When I went to him about the 'gifts,' he did say an attractive woman like me should expect to have men falling at my feet," she recalled. "I didn't take it as a compliment coming from him. In fact, I tried to shrug off the comment. There was always something condescending in his tone when he spoke to me so, no, I never really took that to mean he had a thing for me."

"Guys who stalk women are generally uncomfortable around them in a dating sense. I'm guessing Rod is single," he said.

"You know what? I don't really know. I never asked but I don't remember seeing a band on his finger either," she stated. "I can't recall seeing any wedding pictures in his office. He keeps it tidy. There were neat stacks of papers. Everything seemed to have a place. I don't remember seeing very many personal effects in there."

Harding circled Rod's name before meeting Naomi's gaze.

"I'll add him to our stops," she said after checking her phone. She shook her head. "It's awful to think someone in a security job would pull something like this."

"He might have been gauging your reaction. He could have been jealous when you started dating. I'm guessing the rumor mill picked up on the fact you'd signed up on the dating app," he said as her cheeks flamed on otherwise smooth, silky skin.

"What you just said made something else click," she said. "Rod warned me about dating before I was ready."

"How did you respond?" he asked, more interested than ever in Rod as a suspect.

"I shrugged it off because, now that I think about it, he was known to make comments that I didn't think were completely appropriate at work," she said.

"One reason for not actually putting in better lighting would be to keep his activities in the dark," he stated.

"I should probably know what he drives," she said.

"A truck wouldn't be surprising in these parts," he stated.

"As I recall, the parking lot at the hospital is a sea of trucks, SUVs, and Jeeps," she stated.

"Color can help us rule some out," he said. Or at least, he hoped so. They were narrowing the list as he crossed off a couple of names from the dating site. He'd take the progress however small it might be.

And he had a few choice words for Rod.

———

Harding's overnight improvement was more than Naomi could have hoped for. They were making progress on the case. At least, narrowing down suspects. The sun was shining and it looked like it was shaping up to be a warm day. Plus, the bagels had been pure heaven. Coffee was even better. This should make her feel good. Knowing someone out there had eyes on her and, at the very least, wanted to make her miserable but probably wanted to do worse than that killed any happiness.

After talking to Harding, she had a bad feeling

about Rod. To be fair, she never had liked the guy. Now? He gave her the creeps.

Discussing her horrible dating app dates reminded her just how little she had felt ready to date. Sitting across the table from men she barely knew held no appeal. Being with Harding was easy. Despite knowing him for a short time, being together in his kitchen felt like the most natural thing.

"By the way, this is off the subject, but you shouldn't be hard on yourself about whether or not you put victims at ease," she said. "I barely know you and I was comfortable sleeping in the same room with you last night as well as being alone in your house with you today." She shook her head. "I get along with a lot of people for work but that doesn't mean I want to be around many." She heard the way that sounded. "Or maybe I should say that I prefer to be home watching a movie or reading a book on my days off, over sitting in a crowded room with a stranger."

"I can be accused of the same thing," he stated.

"I noticed how many books you have here," she said, thinking he was a man after her own heart.

"Reading keeps the mind sharp," he said. "It's also a good way to get out of my own head when I'm overthinking a case."

"Makes sense," she said and then studied her screen. They had a lot in common, and in a way she couldn't easily define, almost felt like kindred spirits. "We should probably head out soon."

He nodded as he made a couple of notes on the pad of paper.

"I might need help getting a shirt on," he said when he looked up at her.

"Sounds good," she said, coughing to cover the crick in her throat. "I'll just head upstairs and get ready."

He pushed to standing, using the marble as an anchor.

"Are you alright?" she asked.

"I'll holler if I need you," he said. "Go on and get ready."

The fact he was standing after what he'd been through was nothing short of a miracle.

"Are you sure you want to push yourself like this?" she asked.

"When I was coming out of surgery, I had the scariest few moments of my life when I tried to move and couldn't. The thought of being paralyzed in any way for the rest of my life sent a strong message," he admitted. "In general, I know my body and I know what it can do in a workout. This? It was horrific."

"Is that why you're up and around, pushing yourself?" she asked. "Because you need to feel whole again?"

"Something like that...yes," he said. "The other piece of it is just being grateful for what I can do, and I won't know that unless I find the boundaries."

"I've never met anyone like you before, Harding," she said. The annoying voice in the back of her mind said she never would again. It was right. She knew it. The question was what to do about it.

Naomi headed upstairs where she zipped through the shower, dressed, and applied light makeup. This was the second time in two days she'd bothered with concealer and lip gloss. She stared at the dog tags hanging around her neck in the mirror. Could she take them off?

It might not hurt to leave them on the dresser for safe keeping.

The thought of being without them sent her pulse racing, so she put them in a special pocket in her purse. That way, a piece of Gavin would be with her today. She missed her friend. She missed the person he used to be. She missed the easy-going relationship they'd had in high school. Running into him again had felt like destiny. It was as if the gods themselves had lined up the meeting so the two of them could be together, this time forever. They'd discussed how it must be fate for them to get married after all.

She issued a sharp sigh, no longer believing in the stars lining up or kismet as some called it. People made their own destinies. Period. That was her new mantra. That same annoying voice from a few minutes ago reminded her people had to be brave enough to go for the things they wanted if they wanted to create their own future.

Point taken.

Naomi dressed in a body-hugging jogging suit. She threw on a pair of comfortable sneakers and then pulled her hair off her face in a loose bun before heading downstairs. One look at a shirtless Harding and her pulse kicked up a few notches to say the least. Her attraction to this man was so much more than physical even though his body was made for sin. A physical attraction would never be this strong or have the kind of pull that made it impossible to think about not being around him. Soon enough, she would be back at work, doing twelve-hour shifts and he'd be back to his schedule, which seemed to include a fair amount of travel.

Thinking about what he did for a living stopped her right there. It was so easy to fall for Harding while he was home and they were together. What about when he returned to work? What about when he strapped on a badge and a gun, and headed off to capture some of the world's most dangerous criminals? What kind of life would it be for her wondering every night if he'd come home or show up in the ER at hers or any other hospital? She might not have passion and fireworks in her life right now but she also didn't have to lie awake, staring at the ceiling all night because too many awful images of him lying in a ditch somewhere claimed her thoughts.

No matter how strong a pull she felt toward him, the reality was that she didn't want to spend the rest of her life in fear. Just thinking about it now caused her chest to squeeze and the air to thin. It was like suddenly being shoved underwater with no chance to break the surface. If there was any way to crush those thoughts, those fears, she would do it for Harding. She'd barely gotten through the nightmares in those first couple of months after receiving the news about Gavin. The thought of going through anything close to that again was crippling.

A couple of fortifying breaths later, she coughed to let him know she was walking into the room. She'd learned from her father that it was a bad idea to surprise a man who carried a gun.

"I can help with that," she said to him, motioning toward the pullover shirt he had laid out on the bed.

"Good timing," he said. "I was just about to try on my own, which is probably not a good idea."

Timing had never been her forte. It if was, she wouldn't be falling for a guy she couldn't have after losing one she thought she'd spend the rest of her life alongside. No, she'd never been good with timing and she feared she would pay another hefty price because of it.

CHAPTER FIFTEEN

Harding noticed the lack of dog tags the minute Naomi walked into his bedroom. He took note and moved on, not quite ready to assign a meaning to it. Not ready to assign it hope.

"Let's get your arms in first," she said as her hand came up to his bicep. The now-familiar trill of electricity shot through him, reminding him that he was very much alive and well. The last part was a work in progress but he was healing and could already tell he was gaining strength. He wasn't kidding before when he talked about being shocked out of his mind in those first few moments after the anesthesia started to wear off. He'd also made a promise not to take anything for granted if he got his movement back. Other than being sore, he'd regained movement in both arms and legs. All of the fingers and thumbs on both hands were good. He vowed never to take little things for granted again.

As he shifted and bent forward, his side screamed in pain.

"Are you okay?" she asked.

"You know, I can probably just put on another flannel shirt instead. The buttons would probably work best anyway," he conceded, also grateful Naomi had agreed to come stay with him. She was an incredible nurse and it was easy to see how much she cared about her work. He credited her with the good night of sleep he had last night. It never would have happened without her here.

"That might work best," she agreed. "I'll need to check your wound throughout the day to make sure it's healing right and there's no infection. In fact, we could probably do that before you get a shirt on. I was just going to raise up the hem, but no shirt is good."

He heard her voice crack and could tell the electricity crackling in the air between them was having the same effect on her. At least the attraction wasn't one-sided. It would be unfortunate to be the only one feeling this thing happening between them. It had the force of a tsunami when it hit him square in the chest.

Harding broke eye contact before walking over to his closet. He retrieved a new shirt. "I can get this one on my own. I won't button it yet."

Naomi walked into the bathroom where she still had supplies laid out from last night. He'd let them be. He followed, figuring it would be easier to bring the wound to the care rather than the other way around. But once he stepped inside the bathroom, he realized his mistake. This close in an enclosed space, the smell of her citrusy soap filled his lungs.

She turned around to face him and her violet eyes

glittered with something that looked a whole lot like desire.

"Step closer to me," she said as he watched her pulse race at the base of her throat.

"Kissing again would be a bad idea, wouldn't it?" he asked, the words came out before he had a chance to think about what he was going to say.

"We did say that," she said, and her voice had dropped a few octaves, making it sound even sexier if that was possible. "But I'm having difficulty remembering why at the moment."

"Same here," he admitted as he stared into her beautiful eyes—a beauty that was so much more than skin deep. Physical features were one thing, but when someone's intelligence, compassion, and kindness surpassed the outer shell, then the person truly became beautiful to Harding. He could count on one finger the number of women he'd met who fit that bill to a T. She happened to be standing right in front of him. "I'd like your permission to kiss you."

"Granted," was all she said before they met in the middle.

All reasoning flew out the window the second her lips pressed against his. He could feel her exhale against his mouth and the smell of minty toothpaste mixed with dark roast was too tempting to pass up. He teased his tongue inside her mouth as her fingers came up to grip his shoulders, her fingernails digging into his skin. It was almost as sexy as the way her tongue worked his. One word came to mind. *Home.*

He pulled back and whispered, "I doubt I could ever get enough of you."

"We should go," she said through labored breath. "Even if I don't want to leave."

Those words made his heart sing. He needed to figure out a next step with her because he didn't want this to end in a couple of days. Did she feel the same? Or was he the person who was finally helping her get over Gavin? A one-time fling? Normally, he'd be game but this was different. Naomi was different. She had the ability to rock his world when she walked out.

She smiled at him before redressing his wound. She worked a lot faster than he ever could and it was easy to see that she was skilled at her job.

"All done," she said as she gingerly placed the tape over the gauze.

"Your fingers work magic," he said, capturing her wrist before bringing the tips of her fingers to his lips so he could kiss them.

"Yours aren't so bad either," she stated. "And neither are your lips."

"Before we head down a road we can't finish, we should go," he said, thinking how easy it would be to stay here and get lost in this beauty.

"Right," she agreed on a sigh.

Besides, he didn't want to be the one she used to get over her former boyfriend before walking away forever. Once wouldn't be enough with Naomi, and he needed to know there would be a second time...and a third... and a fourth. Since this line of thinking was as productive as using a glass of water to put out a forest fire, he refocused to the task at hand.

Ten minutes later, they had a small list of addresses and were ready to hit the road. He intended to follow

up with the dating app about her experiences with
Steven and Raul. The site administrator needed to
know how these men were treating dates. Then, there
was Rod, Theo, Dr. Juno, and Sara from work to
consider. Hopefully, their little field trip would narrow
the list further based on what type of vehicles they
drove. Naomi was certain a male had left the note on
her SUV when it was parked in front of his home,
which didn't immediately rule out Sara. Her husband
could have been the one to do it. Or her stepson if he
was old enough. Harding believed he remembered
Naomi mentioning the boy was a teenager. That could
mean a wide range of ages anywhere from thirteen to
nineteen. A thirteen-year-old's strength was a far cry
from someone who was about to turn twenty.

"You drive an SUV, so my truck will have a similar
feel," he stated, handing over the keys.

"I should be okay," she reassured.

"Let's see what your co-workers drive," he said. "I
put the addresses in order while you were upstairs. We
can make a loop."

"Where are we headed first?" she asked.

"Sara's house is up, then Rod's," he said. "Next, we'll
hit Dr. Juno's home before rounding out to Theo's
mother's house. He's the closest to the hospital, so I
figured we would make a nice circle."

"He's at work now, so I hope his mother is home
with their vehicle. Dr. Juno and I have two of the same
days off, today and tomorrow, which doesn't mean that
he's home. Rod works my hours, so he should be off
work. Doesn't mean he'll be home, though."

"It's still worthwhile to swing by his home and check

for a second vehicle. Some folks keep a truck for hauling things but don't use it as their everyday vehicle," he pointed out.

"True," she said. "And it would be smart to use a secondary vehicle to pull something like leaving a note on someone's SUV in broad daylight."

He nodded. She caught on quick. Nurses and U.S. Marshals saw enough of the bad side of people to make them both skeptical and distrustful. It could make trusting difficult, which was another surprise when it came to Naomi. Sleeping in the same room with someone was the ultimate sign of trust. Both had had their best night of sleep in *ages*.

"Let's do this," she said before tossing his key in the air and then catching it again. She shouldered her handbag after tucking her cell phone inside.

He picked up the paper, pad, and a pen once he'd pocketed his own cell.

The drive to Sara's neighborhood didn't take long. Her address was an apartment, so that was going to make pinning down her vehicle that much more difficult. As they turned into the small complex, he realized the task would be impossible. There was a sea of trucks, all makes and models and mostly dark in color, in the lot. The apartments were old and in need of a facelift. A maintenance man tooled around nearby in a golf cart.

"Does Sara work tonight?" he asked.

"Yes, she does," Naomi stated as she slowed down and made a circle. "I was hoping for a complex with attached garages."

"Same here," he admitted. "But that would probably be a little too easy."

"Probably," she agreed.

The maintenance man zipped past. Could they flag him down and get information out of him?

———

"Do you mind pulling over?" Harding asked. Naomi wondered if they had the exact same idea to speak to the maintenance man. The apartment complex was small and she figured maintenance workers would probably know what went on.

"Sure," she said. "Would it be alright if I give it a shot, though?"

"If you're talking about the maintenance man, it can't hurt," he said as the corners of his lips upturned in a grin. "I'll send an inquiry about Raul and Steven to the dating app administrator while you see if you can work some magic."

"Sounds like a plan." She parked in the first available visitor's spot before waving down the golf cart driver.

"Can I help you, ma'am?" he asked. The maintenance man was dressed in a khaki-colored shirt and pants. His nametag was sewn on. It read: Kelly. Kelly was five feet nine inches as a guess. He wasn't built but looked scrappy, like he could handle his own if needed. His smile revealed large teeth and he wore a thick gold chain around his neck. There was dirt under his fingernails, so she figured he was the one who kept things running in the apartments.

"I have a gift for my friend Sara. She lives here with her husband and stepson, and I'm embarrassed to say that I can't remember which truck is hers," Naomi said, figuring the shot in the dark was worth it. He would correct her if she was wrong. "The gift is a surprise. We work together at the hospital, and I noticed she's been down in the dumps lately. Thought I might cheer her up."

"She's not here right now. She normally parks over there," Kelly said. Interesting that he seemed to know when she was around. "Ever since her and her husband split, she isn't home much."

Naomi tried not to hide her shock at the news.

"They've been having trouble," she agreed. "It's the reason she's been depressed lately."

Kelly's eyebrow shot up, and Naomi realized she'd just missed the mark.

"Financially," she clarified. "She said it would be hard on her without his salary."

Kelly nodded.

"Jackson wasn't any good for her. She deserved someone who wouldn't go behind her back with other women while she was at work," he continued. The man really did know everyone's business.

"Then there is his son to consider," she said.

"I feel sorry for him too," Kelly said, delivering another shock. Naomi felt a twinge of guilt for not getting to know her co-worker better. Sara's life had clearly been turned upside-down with a cheating spouse and Naomi hadn't known any different. It explained why Sara had been extra moody at work lately. The pills? She wondered how they fit into the equation. Sara could be taking them for herself. She could be selling them to make ends meet.

"Yeah, poor kid," she said.

"How does a father just walk out on his own son? Leave him with someone who isn't even his mother?" Kelly said with an exacerbated sigh.

Sara clearly had a lot on her plate.

"Thanks for the information," she said. "I'll just surprise her at work."

"The black truck sits right there when she's home in case you want to come back later," Kelly said.

"I will, and thanks again," she stated before saying goodbye and heading back to Harding's vehicle. She reclaimed the driver's seat, put the gearshift in reverse and then backed out of the spot.

"You won't believe this," she said under her breath like Kelly could somehow hear. As soon as she pulled out of the complex, she added, "She drives a black truck."

"Duly noted," he said.

"She is also in the middle of personal drama." She continued by filling him in on what she'd just learned and he agreed about her assumptions on the pills.

"Either way, she is headed down a path that leads to jail time," he stated. "The stepson she seems to care about could end up in foster care."

"I should have asked how old he was, but no, that would be a dead giveaway that I didn't know Sara as well as I was pretending to," she said. "I'm also wondering if her ex is who I've heard her arguing on the phone with recently."

"Could she be in a new relationship already?" Harding asked, putting in the next destination into the GPS.

"Good question," she stated as she navigated toward

Rod's home. "Did you find out anything from the dating app administrator?"

"They couldn't give out information from any of their clients," he said. "At least they had the sense to protect them. I couldn't make the call in an official capacity, so it wasn't like I could push them either."

"Right," she stated. "Too bad I didn't pick Steven up, instead of the other way around."

"Might be a good move in the future," he said. His comment stung.

"Speaking of my place, we were going to swing by to check my upstairs window," she stated, doing her best to cover her disappointment.

"Right. I forgot to mention it, didn't I?" he said. "I meant to work that in after Rod and before Dr. Juno. Did you know the two of you live within a mile of each other?"

"Me and Dr. Juno?" she asked. "Why on earth would he live anywhere near my neighborhood?"

"My mind snaps to a suspicious place, but it could be as simple as proximity to the hospital. Everyone lives relatively close to each other and when I say that, I mean within a fifteen- to twenty-minute drive to work," he said. Still, the news about Dr. Juno living so close caused an icy chill to race down her back.

"He has made off-handed comments about riding to work together," she said. "I thought he was kidding or hinting at the fact he wanted to get to know me better outside of work. It never occurred to me that he could literally walk to my house to catch a ride."

Naomi involuntarily shivered when she thought about some of the other comments he'd made.

CHAPTER SIXTEEN

GPS indicated Rod's house was coming up on the left. Naomi had been quiet ever since learning the news about Dr. Juno's residence. It was cause for alarm for Harding. He could almost hear the wheels churning in her mind and she'd gone inside herself again, shutting out the world. A sure sign another wall came up.

He shelved his frustration, wishing she would let him in this time. But what was he offering in return? And would she even be willing to risk dating while she was going through this? Her trust in men couldn't exactly be high right now and yet what the two of them shared was different.

The dating app administrator's response to his inquiry had been a disappointment. Those men dropped low on the suspect list so he wouldn't push. With the rumors going around at work, though, he thought about the saying, *where there's smoke, there's fire.* Signs pointed to this being personal and he couldn't help but think the dates didn't have that much of an attachment after an express rejection from Naomi. He could be wrong and the trail needed to be followed but the priority was low. Instincts kept pointing to this being a personal crime and experience said most crimes against women fell into that category.

Naomi slowed the vehicle to a crawl as they passed by the home. It was brick with a concrete slab porch. The door was painted white and the yard was mowed. There was a chain-link fence around the front of the yard and a gate in a similar style. Trees dotted the street and the sidewalk was cracked as a result but there were none in the front yard at least. The house was nondescript and there was essentially no landscaping to speak of. It looked like a bachelor could live there.

"No garage," Naomi said.

"None," he agreed. "And no truck."

There was, however, a mint green Dodge parked out front. Roommate? Harding took note of the license plate, just in case they needed to reference the vehicle later. If it showed up, he would know if it was the same one. There weren't a whole lot of mint green Dodges being driven around but being thorough meant leaving nothing to chance.

"Figuring out what he drives might not be the easiest thing at the hospital even if we stop by tonight," Naomi admitted. "I can always ask around once I start my shift or we could sit in the parking lot and wait for him to show."

Harding hoped to have a name before she went back to work. It might be ambitious but she was in more danger with each passing day. The stalker had moved from leaving 'gifts' at her job, to making a demand while she was parked in front of his home. A thought struck that someone from work would also know his background and what he did for a living. The person was bold and becoming bolder.

Naomi's cell phone rang.

"Do you want me to check it?" he asked. It was the least he could do since she was the one driving.

"Please," she said, nudging her handbag with her elbow.

He reached in and pulled out the phone before checking the screen.

"Theo," he said.

She immediately pulled over and parked on the side street in time to answer before the call rolled into voicemail.

"Hi, Theo," she stated, hitting the speaker button so Harding could hear.

"I'm s-s-s-orry," Theo said. "Please don't h-hate me. I feel so bad for what he asked me to do. He said it was for your own good and that I'd be helping you. He said you were going to get fired if you kept it up. But now you don't like me anymore. You're not my friend and—"

"Theo, we're still friends, okay?" Naomi's voice was a study in calm. "Nothing can change that."

"You're not mad for what I d-did?" he stammered.

"I'm not thrilled but friends can be upset with each other and still be friends," she explained.

"Mother says it's important to say you're sorry," he continued, seeming relieved.

"She is right," Naomi said. "And just so we're on the same page, what exactly are you apologizing for?"

"Going into the room the other night," he said. "And then yesterday after work. Following you was wrong. I wanted to help."

"When did you start driving?" Naomi asked.

"Mother lets me drive sometimes," he admitted.

"You know it's illegal without a driver's license," she said. "You could get into trouble with the police. We wouldn't want that."

"No. I would lose my job," he said. "I don't know what I would do without going to work."

"And we need you there too," she continued. "You're a valuable employee and we wouldn't be able to do what we do without you."

"I like to work," he said.

"Theo, who told you to follow me?" she asked.

"He did," he said like it was as obvious as the noses on their faces.

"Who is he?" she pressed.

"I'm not really supposed to tell," he said.

"I won't tell anyone," she stated, feeling awful for the deception.

"He'll get mad, and he said if he got mad that he might come to my house and hurt Mother." The worry in Theo's voice stabbed Harding in the center of the chest.

"What if I tell you that I can talk to him and make sure that doesn't happen?" Naomi asked.

"No. No. He's important. He has an important job and he keeps us all safe," he said. "I-I gotta go."

Before she could continue, Theo hung up.

"We have to go to his house so I can speak to him in person," she stated. "I know if I saw him face-to-face, I could get answers out of him."

"I don't think it's a good idea," he said. "He might call the person he referenced to apologize."

"True," she said. "It did seem important to him." She paused a couple of beats. "He mentioned the person responsible keeps us safe. I'm guessing that means Rod."

"I definitely have questions for him," Harding stated. "Let's swing by your place and check the window."

———

Naomi lived in a small three-building apartment complex on Apple Grove Drive. She parked on the street down the block rather than announce her arrival by parking in her usual spot. She might be in a truck but she wouldn't take any chances. Her particular unit had two floors and there were times when she left the upstairs window cracked to let fresh air in.

As soon as she exited the vehicle, Harding came around to the driver's side and clasped their hands. The connection gave her the confidence to keep going when a growing piece of her wanted to bolt. Running from a problem never made it better, she reminded, so she tightened her grip around Harding's hand. The now-familiar jolt of electricity that came with contact comforted her.

Thankfully, the area was quiet and there didn't seem to be any peering eyes watching them. Theo's words sat heavy on her chest and she hated the fact he'd been used by someone at work. The suspect list shortened real fast with his admission. This had to be the workings of someone at work. Theo mentioned a *he*. That pretty much ruled out Sara unless her soon-to-be-ex or stepson was involved. At the very least, the hospital needed to be made aware of her actions when it came to taking patients' meds.

Naomi unlocked the door and then they both slipped inside. Harding closed and locked the door behind them.

"Does anything look out of the ordinary?" he immediately asked, back against the door. He'd reached for a weapon almost the second he'd let go of her hand so she could get her house key out of her purse.

"Not down here. No," she said, scanning the living room, dining room, and most of the kitchen. Someone could be hunkered down behind the cabinets, but she could see most of the rooms from this vantage point. There was a counter-height bar that blocked part of the view to the kitchen. With Harding taking the lead, they moved toward it.

"It's clear," he said after rounding the corner from the dining room and thoroughly investigating the kitchen and pantry.

"Upstairs?" she asked but it was more statement than question.

Harding nodded before, again, leading the way. They cleared the hall closet, second bedroom that she used as a small office, and then the master.

"He's gone," she said as she motioned toward the window that was opened large enough for a person to fit through. "He would have had to jump from the window. There's no way he could have closed it behind him."

Harding walked over to the sill and studied it. "Fingers gripped here." He pointed as she joined him.

Sure enough, the marks of hands holding on probably for dear life as he lowered himself enough to drop were visible.

"How did he climb out and not leave much of a trail?" she asked. Then again, the window was open wide enough to drive a truck through. Okay, a truck was an exaggeration. The window wasn't that big.

"I'm guessing he came out on his side," he said, motioning toward a spot that was about six inches wide in the center.

"Makes sense," she stated.

"If this was an official investigation, I would dust for prints," Harding said.

"We can't prove anyone was here," she said. "An opened window isn't exactly illegal activity."

"I'm wondering how he got inside," Harding said. "We should check the windows downstairs."

"It's possible he used a ladder," she said. "If he had on anything that looked like a work uniform, he could slip right in unnoticed. People mind their own business in this complex."

"If someone gives the impression they belong somewhere, people generally take it on face value," he said.

"Sounds about right," she agreed. "Also, if it is Rod and he was wearing his uniform..."

"People would really look the other way," he said.

"They might even smile at him," she added. The thought of Rod being in her apartment and rummaging through her things gave her the creeps. Naomi involuntarily shivered at the thought. If this was the case, she had a few choice words for the man. But why come into her apartment? "Do you think he was trying to surprise me?"

"The message to go home yesterday was definitely meant to get you out of my place," Harding reasoned.

"True," she said.

"But there's another reason he would come here if he knew you were gone," he continued. "Someone who develops a fixation might break in to take a personal belonging of the object of their affection."

That really made a cold chill race down her spine.

"As in...underwear?" she asked, realizing she might not want to know the answer to her question.

"Could be. I've heard of a favorite piece of jewelry being taken. Earrings. A necklace someone wears often or holds a special meaning," he said. "Or an article of clothing."

Naomi raced to her underwear drawer and then opened it. She had a whole organization system that came in handy now. "Nothing in here has been disturbed."

"Laundry basket?" he asked.

She might actually become sick at the thought of someone like Rod stealing underwear from the wash.

"Please, no," she said as she practically bolted into the master bath and to the basket she kept there. She dug around inside the full basket. "Today would have been laundry day."

Harding leaned against the doorframe, looking like he needed to sit.

"Do you want a chair?" she asked.

"No. I'm fine," he said with a quick head shake. "Don't worry about me."

How could she not? His skin paled and he shouldn't be moving around this much. "Are you sure?"

Harding nodded.

As she picked through the basket, she realized what was missing. "I have a Tiffany blue velvet jogging suit. It's my favorite and I usually wear it on my day off, except I changed at work the other day because I had to run a few errands. When my shift is done, I have to get out of my scrubs unless I'm going straight home."

"He must have seen you wearing them," Harding said.

"I hope that's the case," she said. "Otherwise, he watches me on my day off."

Another involuntary shiver rocked her body at the thought.

"If nothing else is missing, we should head back to the house," he stated. "Rod's not due to the hospital for a few hours and I should probably get off my feet for a little while after we eat. Save up strength for our visit to the hospital later."

"Okay," she said before bolting into her bedroom to close and lock the window. "Once we make sure all the windows are secure downstairs first."

Naomi couldn't find the words to describe how violated she felt at the reality of someone breaking into her home, rummaging through her belongings, and stealing her worn clothes. Had her instincts been right the other night too? Had Rod been watching her as she parked her SUV in the lot? As she'd walked in the dark toward the hospital?

His insistence that she was overreacting to the lack of lighting, to the 'gifts' made a whole lot more sense to her now. What else was he planning?

CHAPTER SEVENTEEN

A nap followed by an early dinner had Harding back on his feet. The realization of theft at Naomi's earlier meant the stalker's acts were escalating. Not a good sign and still nothing that could be proven to the law. Stalking cases were considered gray area and, plus, there was no concrete evidence to go on. They would get it, though, at the hospital.

Harding glanced over at the clock as he stretched his muscles. They screamed, so he cooled it. Taking on Naomi's case while he was less than his best physically shouldn't pose a problem at this point. Going to her workplace should be safe enough. He had a license to carry and a badge to back it up, so he figured they were in good shape. He hoped he wouldn't need to get physical with anyone.

Sounds from the next room said she was up and moving around. He forced himself to sit up before throwing his legs over the side of the bed. The light was on in the bathroom and the door was cracked. Naomi seemed to have left him a trail to follow.

Before he could stand up, she appeared in the doorway and the smell of coffee assaulted him.

"How did you know I was up?" he asked, a little in shock.

"You started stirring, so I figured it was only a matter of time," she admitted with a smile that lit a dozen campfires low in his stomach.

"You're even more beautiful when you smile," he said before catching himself. This wasn't the time to point out how much he wanted to walk over and kiss her, or the fact that she was stunningly beautiful. Especially after what they'd discovered at her apartment. "What I should ask is if you're doing okay."

"What you said first was nice," she said with another warm smile that caused his chest to squeeze.

"Thank you for the coffee," he said.

"I'll set it down here on the nightstand for when you get out of the bathroom," she said as a red blush crawled over her cheeks. He dipped his gaze to the base of her neck and relief washed over him when he saw the chain with dog tags was still gone. Could he compete with her past? He hoped so, because he'd never fallen for someone so fast and so fully. It seemed a shame not to figure out what that could mean.

After freshening up in the bathroom, he walked back into the bedroom. The lights were on now and he was fully awake. He took a couple sips of coffee before dressing with Naomi's help. Her hands trembled but she kept her chin up.

"How are you really doing?" he asked as he leaned against the bed and sipped the dark roast.

"Nervous," she said. "Shocked."

"You're doing great," he said.

"I have a lot of experience shoving my true emotions down somewhere deep," she said, holding out a shaky hand. "Clearly, I haven't gotten all the way there with the Rod situation."

"Fear makes us human," he said.

"Are you ever afraid of anything?" she asked, incredulous.

"Of course," he said. "Fear keeps me alive. It makes my senses sharp and tells me when I'm in danger. Recent event aside, my instincts have an amazing track record. Plus, fear is what caused me to duck before I even heard the shotgun blast."

She moved beside him and then smoothed her hand against the injury.

"I, for one, am happy you listened," she stated. This felt like the most intimate moment in Harding's life, which was strange considering they were both fully dressed. But there was something very personal in sharing memories, a space, and in this case, even a cup of coffee.

Since they were close and he wanted to end this nightmare for her once and for all, he set his cup down and pushed to standing. "Ready to head out when you are."

"Let's go," she said, sounding a little more confident and a little less resigned. "I'd like to put this chapter behind me."

"Agreed," was all he said because they couldn't turn

the page until she was free from this situation. Then, he wanted to have a conversation about possibilities between them if any existed on her side.

They walked into the garage, hand in hand like it was the most natural thing. The drive to the hospital took a while. Silence sat between them. Not the awkward silence of strangers but of two people who were comfortable in each other's company without the need to fill the space with words.

She parked in the lot by the ER bay. He exited the truck, linked their fingers, and walked toward the bright light of the hospital. This area was black as pitch. Harding couldn't believe security didn't take her seriously because it would be so easy to grab an unsuspecting person from this lot. He shelved those thoughts for now, wanting to feel Rod out and get a sense if the guy fit the profile. Sara would be a good one to interview next and she should be on shift. She seemed eager to take over for Naomi the other night, but then she might have been trying to get her hands on Percocet.

Inside, Naomi walked them down the hallway. The white tile flooring and walls could use some color to make the place less sterile. Harding made a note to mention the hospital at his family's annual charity meeting. Maybe they would be willing to fund a few updates.

After several turns, Naomi badged them inside a small hallway. Stepping inside was walking into gray walls and floors, and away from the light. A few steps in and they stood in front of a door that read *Head of Security* along with the name *Rod Ager*.

Naomi knocked.

"Come in," came a distracted male voice. His gaze

widened when he saw Harding enter behind Naomi. "What's going on? This is your day off?"

"Mind if we ask a couple of questions?" Harding started in.

"Why?" Rod's nose wrinkled like he'd just smelled his own backside after passing gas. The guy's initial reaction and overall demeanor didn't exactly fit the profile of a quiet guy who is intimidated to speak to women. Rod was an obnoxious jerk.

"Can we sit down?" Naomi asked, motioning toward the chairs opposite Rod's desk. There wasn't a whole lot of room but Naomi would easily fit.

"Do what you want," Rod said, leaning back in his chair, forcing it onto two legs. The office was barely large enough to fit the three of them, his desk, and a plastic floor plant. The metal and vinyl seats weren't the sturdiest. He clasped his hands behind his head. "Are you here to complain about lighting again? Brought reinforcements?"

"I'd rather ask what kind of vehicle you drive," she stated, but she was on the wrong track.

Harding reached for her hand after they sat down. He used his index finger to stroke the inside of her hand. She gave a slight nod and he hoped she got the message. Rod wasn't their guy. At least, not on the surface.

"I'm in a sedan right now," he admitted, looking a little embarrassed. "Had to borrow my sister's car while mine is in the shop."

Naomi glanced over at Harding before locking gazes with Rod. She leaned forward. "You know, the real reason I'm here is out of concern for Theo. He's been acting strange lately and I just wanted to see if you'd noticed."

Rod took his time looking from Harding to Naomi.

"Looks like the rumor is true. You're dating patients," he said. It took all Harding's strength not to come across the desk after the smirk on Rod's face.

"This is my friend," she corrected. "Our families go way back."

"Is that so?" Rod asked, looking like he didn't believe a word. The man didn't seem like the brightest bulb in the box and none of Harding's danger signals flared in Rod's company. Between those and the fact Rod didn't fit the profile, Harding realized they were back at the drawing board.

"Suffice it to say that we know each other," Harding said to Rod, who suddenly squirmed in his seat when Harding spoke up.

"Okay," Rod said.

"You know what," Naomi said, seeming to catch on, "I need to find Theo. Have you seen him around?"

"You might want to check on five," Rod said. "That's where he was the last time I saw him."

Naomi managed to squeeze behind Harding.

"Are you two all good without me?" she asked when Harding didn't stand.

"Yes," he said. "We're going to come up with a plan for parking lot lighting. Right, Rod?"

"Whatever you say," Rod quipped, but the man seemed to know when he'd been outmaneuvered. Refusing to take Naomi's complaints seriously now would create liability. Rod didn't want that.

"I'll catch up with you in a few minutes," Naomi said.

"Be there in a few minutes," he stated as she walked out the door. Once in the hallway and out of Rod's sight, she stopped long enough to turn and wink. His chest squeezed before he turned his attention toward Rod. "Talk to me about why you seem so adamant about refusing a female employee's request for proper lighting in the parking lot."

Rod balked. This was going to be a fun conversation. It was about time this jerk faced some accountability.

———

Naomi strode to the elevator with renewed purpose. Theo would come clean if she was able to get him one on one for a few minutes. He knew who was behind the threats to her and this situation needed to end today. Breaking into her home crossed a line. Stealing her personal belongings crossed a line. Pretending any of this was being done for her own good crossed a line.

The elevator doors opened almost immediately after she hit the button. She palmed her phone figuring it might be easier to request Theo meet her in the cafeteria. She pushed the button going to five just in case he didn't have his cell in hand. Either way, she planned to get him to talk. Harding would be joining her in a few minutes and she hoped to have information to share.

The look on Rod's face when Harding said he was sticking around in the man's office had been priceless. Naomi figured lights would be going up in the next few days if Harding had anything to say about it.

Someone having her back was a nice change of pace. She could get used to this...to him. Was it time to move on from the past and start thinking about her future? A small voice in the back of her mind pointed out Gavin would want her to be happy. Could she allow it?

The elevator dinged and she exited on five. As she rounded the corner, a figure ran right into her. The person had something covering their face and she was hit with the kind of force that almost knocked her on her backside. Naomi lost her balance, reaching out for the wall behind her to steady herself so she didn't fall.

"Excuse me," she mumbled but the person barreled into her, shoving her into a closet. The light flicked off as she struggled against the person who seemed determined to knock her out.

"Mine," was all the familiar voice said as a cloth came over her mouth and a chemical smell engulfed her.

"No," she argued, ramming an elbow into Jeffrey Juno's body. She couldn't see well enough to aim for his face but the grunt was satisfying as she made contact.

"If I can't have you, no one ever will," he whispered and there was something sinister in his voice now.

Naomi figured she had a couple of seconds before the chemical knocked her out. That had to be his plan. Make her compliant and then what? Kill her? "You won't get away with this," she managed to say as she fought against the cloth being secured over her nose and mouth. Juno was surprisingly strong for a man of his stature. But then, he had a lot to lose right now.

She drew her knee up as hard as she could, connecting with his groin.

"Bitch," Juno shouted and there was an ominous tone in his voice.

Naomi capitalized on the moment and screamed for help. Almost instantly, the door swung open and the light came on. A second later, Harding dove into Juno.

"Get out of here and get help," he said to Naomi, creating enough of a distraction for her to break out of Juno's grasp. She managed to fumble for her cell phone and sent a text to Rod as Harding pinned Juno between his legs.

"She belongs to me," Juno said, frantic now.

Naomi turned in time to see him fist a needle. "Watch out, Harding."

As Juno's hand reared back, Harding caught the man's wrist.

"Not today, jerk," Harding said as he squeezed Juno's wrist so tightly the doctor dropped the needle.

A second later, the elevator doors opened and Rod came bolting out. Naomi was already on her cell to 911. She gave a two-second rundown to Rod as he practically bolted into the supply closet.

Rod cursed.

"You're bleeding," he said to Harding.

Naomi shifted position to get a clear view. Sure enough, Harding's shirt was soaked with blood.

"Secure the needle," Harding said to Rod in an authoritative voice that left no room for question.

Rod complied.

"Put the evidence in a safe place," Harding instructed.

Much to her surprise, Rod seemed eager to help. His widened gaze was a sharp contrast to the looks he'd been giving them downstairs. She had no idea what Harding had said to the security guard, but it had worked. Rod seemed ready to be deputized on the spot.

The hallway started filling with a crowd as a pediatric doctor came running.

"We need help," Naomi said to Dr. Dryden. She nodded as Rod placed handcuffs on Juno.

"I'll be back for you," he said to Naomi as she took a couple of steps backward. "Mark my words."

"The only place you're going is to jail," she said to him. "And, by the way, I think they'll love a soft guy like you where you're going. I have a feeling you'll be very popular with the other inmates."

Juno practically sneered at her. He'd always been a little creepy. Next time she got a similar feeling around someone, she had no plans to write it off.

Harding made his way to Naomi through the small crowd that had gathered. "Are you hurt?"

"No," she said, thinking it was now or never. She had feelings for Harding that she'd never experienced before. "But I could be. By you. Let's get you looked at."

"A couple of stitches popped," he said as Dr. Dryden asked him to pull up his shirt. He did and his assessment was correct.

"I need to get him into a room *now,*" Dr. Dryden ordered. She'd always been no-nonsense, but her stock just went up with Naomi. The woman knew how to command a room.

A couple of nurses scurried around Harding, urging him toward the nearest room. It was empty and he eased onto the table.

"Stay right here?" he asked.

"You couldn't get rid of me if you tried," she said to him as she rounded the bed and took his hand in hers while the doctor and nurses worked their magic.

"That's good to know because I'd like you to stick around for a long time," he said, wincing as the doctor inserted a small needle to numb the area on his side. "In fact, I was thinking of offering permanent closet space if living with me doesn't sound like a bad idea."

"I'd move in with you for the bagels alone," she quipped as her heart literally sang.

He laughed, winced, and then shook his head.

"Figures, it was the bagels," he said with a smile. "But I want you to know that I mean forever. I love you and I want to make us permanent."

"Good," she said, unable to contain her smile. "Because I'm in love with you too. And I've never felt this way about anyone else. Forever seems like a good place to start."

Naomi leaned over and kissed her man, her love, her home.

"I love you," he whispered in her ear.

"With all my heart," she said. "And everything that I am. I love you, Harding Quinn."

And now, she'd found the one place she should be. With Harding. The man she intended to spend the rest of her life with.

CHAPTER EIGHTEEN

Epilogue

Barrett Quinn had seen it all now. He never thought he'd see the day when his brother Harding got down on one knee and proposed. Harding had found the love of his life, and Barrett was genuinely happy for his brother and future bride. The old saying *not losing a brother but gaining a sister* came to mind. Naomi was perfect for Harding. She couldn't be more down-to-earth or a better fit. Good for them.

Seeing them together almost made Barrett wonder what it would be like to divorce his committed bachelor lifestyle and think about tying the knot. Almost.

Barrett almost laughed out loud as he waited in line for his morning bagel and coffee run before work. Friday morning bagels and coffee before work with Harding was one of many rituals Barrett would miss. At least he still got the bagel even if he stood in line alone.

The new relationship would put a crimp in Barrett's plans. Him and his brother were best friends, both U.S. Marshals, and spent much of their time off together.

The fishing, camping, and taking off on a dime days were over. Harding had another person in his life now to consider and it was probably high time he settled down. He'd been different lately. There'd been less enthusiasm in his voice when they made plans.

Still. Barrett would miss their carefree days and buddying around with his sibling.

R.I.P. single life, brother.

Barrett's cell phone buzzed. Since he was up next to order and he didn't want to be rude, he ignored it. Everything could wait until he got his first cup of coffee. Besides, it was probably one of those 'helpful' calls about making sure he extended his car warranty. There'd been a rash of those lately and he was to the point of being ready to toss his cell phone in the garbage and go back to scribbling messages on walls in the form of hieroglyphics. A few caveman jokes came to mind but Barrett had no one to tell them to. He sighed.

Life was changing and he needed to get with the program.

"A bagel and cup of drip," he said to the order taker.

"Single?" she asked.

"Yes, just one," he said a little more defensively than was probably necessary. He almost asked if she saw anyone else standing there with him but stopped himself. The barely twenty-something didn't deserve to be on the receiving end of his grumpiness.

His cell buzzed again, and again more persistently this time.

Barrett plastered on a smile for the worker as he paid. He made sure to thank her in as pleasant a voice as he could rally. She offered a quick smile in return before her eyes shifted to the person behind him in line.

That was Barrett's cue to move it along to the Order Pick-up end of the counter. He did as he fished his cell phone out of his pocket. Calls followed by texts were not a good sign.

The texts were from his supervisor.

Joe Horowitz has escaped Hunstville and was last seen heading in your direction. You are officially on leave. Get out of town a.s.a.p.!

Dirty Joe had murdered two U.S. Marshals before Barrett tracked him down in a South American jungle, put handcuffs on him, and brought him in to face his long list of crimes. Most of the felons Barrett arrested made it known they weren't real pleased with him. None caused Barrett to lose sleep at night, except one. Dirty Joe had vowed to put Barrett six feet under. And he was the only one capable of following through.Every U.S. Marshal had an emergency exit plan they never expected to need. Barrett's just became a reality.

Click here to read the rest of Barrett's story.

ALSO BY BARB HAN

Endangered Heiress

Texas Grit

Kidnapped at Christmas

Murder and Mistletoe

Bulletproof Christmas

For more of Barb's books, visit www.BarbHan.com.

ABOUT THE AUTHOR

Barb Han is a USA TODAY and Publisher's Weekly Bestselling Author. Reviewers have called her books "heartfelt" and "exciting."

Barb lives in Texas--her true north--with her adventurous family, a poodle mix and a spunky rescue who is often referred to as a hot mess. She is the proud owner of too many books (if there is such a thing). When not writing, she can be found exploring Manhattan, on a mountain either hiking or skiing depending on the season, or swimming in her own backyard.

www.ingramcontent.com/pod-product-compliance
Lightning Source LLC
Chambersburg PA
CBHW051955220626
47052CB00004B/950